THE *Dead* ARE RESTING

A NOVEL

Julie Tulba

ISBN-13: 9781733911825

Cover design by Damonza
Cover image: Nazi officers and female auxiliaries (Helferinnen) pose on a wooden bridge in Solahütte © United States Holocaust Memorial Museum
Formatting by Polgarus Studio

Printed in the United States of America

For UB, who made it possible for me to fly.

AUTHOR'S DISCLAIMER:

"When the dead is at rest, let his remembrance rest."

Ecclesiasticus 38:23

 PROLOGUE

Solahütte
Porąbka Village, Poland
July 1944

"So how do you like it here so far?"

The elbow to his ribs from Georg, his new friend of just a few short weeks, startled Max from his reverie.

"I'm sorry, what?" Max asked, glancing in the direction of the young woman who had asked the question but whose name he had already entirely forgotten. Inge? Ilse? Max was silently cursing himself for not being able to remember the name of a girl with such a pretty face. Of which he also noted, there was such a great abundance here at Solahütte.

"Dagmar here was just asking how you were liking it so far," Georg told him.

"Dagmar," he said to himself. Where on earth had I gotten Inge and Ilse from? he thought. Sitting up from his haunches he replied, "Oh, I'm enjoying it a great deal. I find the work challenging but fulfilling, although are there typically so many transports in a given week?" He posed this question to no one in particular since Georg, Oskar, and Johannes but also the girls, the ten *Helferinnen*, knew and were paramount to the camp's operations.

"Not typically," Johannes replied rather lackadaisically, having answered the question with his eyes closed, his hands behind his head, lying back on the picnic blanket as if he were having the most delicious slumber. "But," he continued, "it was time we dealt with the issue of the Hungarian *Judenschwein* once and for all." Johannes was the most senior officer of their small contingent even if he behaved like the most juvenile of schoolboys. Max had lost count of the number of times he had seen him pinching (and trying to pinch) the bottoms of the *Helferinnen* even if the girls had never seemed to mind, only ever playfully swatting away Johannes' hand from their rears.

"Hey, no more talk of work," one of the curly haired *Helferinnen* whom Max had christened Christa because she reminded him of his cousin Christa, an imp of a thing, demanded. "We're supposed to be having fun," and with that she grabbed Johannes' cap, which had been resting on the ground next to him and took off, leaving him with no choice but to follow in close laughing pursuit, the sound of the river's flowing waters able to be faintly heard in the distance.

Hours later, once their small group had fully exhausted themselves against the backdrop of the picturesque setting, signs of the late summer's setting sun nearing, they were about to turn in when Johannnes called out, "Wait, let's get a picture of everyone," having noticed the Kodak Vigilant Junior six-20 camera that Max had had with him all afternoon.

The group congregated together on the little footbridge, Johannes smack in the center with all the *Helferinne* flocking him (naturally, Max thought), Georg on the right even posing with his accordion, having played countless tunes to their group throughout the day, when all of a sudden Johannes said, "Oskar, you take the photo and Max, you stand where Oskar was." Max started to object, not feeling he had earned the right to be in this photo when he was such a newcomer, but Johannes ignored his protestations as did Oskar, who silently but gently took the camera out of Max's hands and went to stand where only a moment before Max had been.

Max awkwardly joined the group, inching closer when Oskar called, "Max, get closer to Liesl, you're not on focus," not wanting to touch, still feeling a bit shy of girls even though he was nearly 23. But almost three years spent fighting on the barbaric wastelands of the Eastern Front and then recuperating in military hospitals from wounds he had sustained in battle, well, there hadn't been a lot of opportunity for finding true love or even just heavy flirting.

"Okay," Oskar cried out, "*eins...zwei...drei...*say cheese."

The group in unison called out "cheese," their smiles and gaiety visible on their faces, some of them laughing so hard they had tears forming in their eyes. They were so busy having such a wonderful time of themselves that none of them noticed the heavy bands of smoke that were rising above the tree lines just a short distance away.

Part I

Becky & Judy

# CHAPTER 1

Pittsburgh, Pennsylvania
2006

Becky's decision to go to Germany, the land of her father's birth and childhood, was how their cold war began. Or as her father referred to Germany, "that place."

"You go to that place you might as well be spitting on the memory of the six million who were murdered," he told her the first time she mentioned she was interested in traveling to Germany. Or when she had told him she was just going to be visiting Munich and Berlin "this time," he had said she was a "*meshuggener*" although unlike when her *bubbe* had called her that, her father was not calling her a crazy fool with any trace of affection. And when the time came where she affixed her itinerary to his refrigerator while he sat at the kitchen table watching her, he solemnly said with an air of resignation, "ka, was my own story, my own hellish experience not enough of a lesson for you? There's so much of the world to see. Why do want to see the one place that tried and almost succeeded in completely destroying our people?"

She had no answer to that, as he knew she wouldn't. So she just kissed the top of his head and left, calling over her shoulder with the words, "I'll call you tomorrow."

Her entire life she had been known as Becky but to her father she was and always would be Rivka, the Hebrew name for Rebecca. Growing up, her father liked to tell people that he had chosen the name Rivka because in Hebrew it means "a woman who takes a man's heart" and that's exactly what she had done the first time he saw her in the hospital.

It had bothered Becky a lot growing up, that her father wouldn't call her by the American version of her name. It wasn't enough that she already felt different being the only one in her class whose dad had that "tattoo" on his arm. But then he had to go and call her a name that sounded like it belonged to an old woman living in a 19th century *shtetl*, and not one living in 1960s Pittsburgh.

"Why can't you just call me Becky like everyone else? I'm an American, I deserve to be called by my AMERICAN name," she remembered yelling at her father one time during a fight in her adolescent years, saying this as if her constitutional rights were being infringed upon.

"Because that's not your name. Your name is Rivka and you are the descendent of Abraham and Sarah, not Paul and Yoko," he told her just as heatedly, not caring or realizing that one, they weren't exactly "related" to Abraham and Sarah and two, Paul and Yoko weren't a thing, at least not according to Dick Clark when she was able to sneak watching American Bandstand.

But Becky's mom, Judy, got it. She'd understood her daughter's wish to just want to fit in and not stand out, as she herself was the daughter of Lithuanian immigrants and knew all too well the callousness and sometimes cruelty of children when you had parents who were "different" and thus treated you differently.

Becky's mom had grown up in a strict Orthodox Jewish household in Pittsburgh's Squirrel Hill neighborhood in the 1930s, which she would tell Becky was like a *shtetl* as a means of making Becky feel better, letting her know that things really weren't "so" bad with her father compared to how it had been during her own childhood. When she was a girl, her mother went to the *mikvah* each month following the end of her menstrual cycle, she couldn't venture beyond the *eruv* even though she longed to go to the pictures or see a game at Forbes Field, and when she really wanted to make Becky smile, she would remind her about the weekly *kishke* that she was expected to eat. When Becky asked the first time what it was, since everything her *bubbe* made was delicious, Judy replied with a straight face and said, "beef intestine stuffed with a seasoned filling." Thankfully even when *bubbe* had come to live with them, *kishke* never made an appearance. And Becky made a point to ask every…time…she saw a foreign looking dish on the dinner table.

Judy had contracted polio as a child and although she had recovered from it, her right foot was permanently disfigured, causing her to walk with a limp, thus rendering her "unmatachable" by the *shadchan*, the religious matchmaker. So her sisters Zipporah and Bina were married off to Jewish men (naturally from Suwalk, the same Lithuanian region their parents had come from), and her brother Moshe matched with a girl from Suwalk. Her mother Yehudit (or Judy as she preferred to be called, being a first generation American and the only one of the four siblings born in America), was left alone, which suited her just fine, knowing she would never need to shave her head and wear the *sheitel*, the wig that Orthodox Jewish married women had to wear in order to confirm with the requirements of Jewish law to cover their hair, or have to go to the *mikvah* each month to get clean so she could lie with her husband once more, or be told she couldn't read a book that wasn't the Torah. She had even convinced her parents to allow her to volunteer at the Irene Kauffman Settlement on Centre Avenue in the city's Hill District. It was through her volunteer work there that she got to know and greatly admire Zena Saul and Anna Heldman, two women who worked tirelessly their entire careers on behalf of the city's populations in need. And her volunteer work also served as the perfect cover when she made plans with her Gentile girlfriends to catch pictures at the Fulton, girls she had gotten to know outside of the *eruv*.

So when Judy ended up meeting and falling in love with a German Jewish refugee who had just arrived in Pittsburgh, a survivor of "the camps," at one of the dances the Friendship Club held, no one batted an eye. They were just happy that Yehudit had found herself a nice Jewish man, even if he was German AND raised as a Reformed Jew AND didn't speak a word of Yiddish. Someone had wanted to marry poor little Yehudit, lame leg and all.

⚜ CHAPTER 2 ⚜

Pittsburgh, Pennsylvania
1950

"Would you like to dance?" a man said in slightly accented English.

Judy hadn't seen the tall, skinny man with big ears and dark blond hair approach her. She had been too busy attempting to work on her British accent so that whenever she met Laurence Olivier he would undoubtedly be impressed by it.

"Sure, if you don't mind my lame leg," drawing her leg out from under the table so he could see the disfigured foot.

He seemed at first like he was going to politely refuse (like most men did when they saw her foot) but then thought better of it and replied, "not at all." Extending his hand towards hers, he helped her up and led her to the dance floor when the sounds of "I'm in the Mood for Love" started to play.

"You're lucky," she said playfully.

"How's that?" he asked, just as playfully as he led her around the floor.

"You got a slow song right off the bat," she told him. "I have the slow dance routine pretty much set but all bets are off when a fast movin' Glenn Miller song comes on."

"I shall keep that in mind," he said, his tone serious, but his twinkling eyes saying otherwise.

When the song ended, he held out his hand and said, "I'm Sam."

"Judy," she told him. "Well, really my name is Yehudit but I prefer Judy. My father's from the Old Country, Pittsburgh's very own Tevye the Dairyman."

He looked at her blankly, clearly waiting for her to explain.

"You know, "she said, slightly flabbergasted that someone who was at a Friendship Club event wouldn't know who Tevye was, "the narrator from Sholem Aleichem's short stories." At his blank look she added, "the famous Yiddish playwright and author?"

"I am sorry, I am not familiar with this Tevye but Yehudit is quite beautiful," he told her.

She thought for a moment he might be joking, having been mocked before for her name by Gentile children, but she could tell he was serious.

"Thank you," she replied. An awkward silence descended over them until she asked what had been on her mind even since he had extended his arm to hers, his shirtsleeve on his left arm creeping up ever so slightly. "You were in the camps?"

He looked stricken, almost as if he would flee from the dance immediately. But then he said, "Shall we get some air?"

And so when they were outside he told her. He told her how when the Nazis first came to power in 1933, no one in his family had believed they were anything more than schoolyard bullies with their big talk and vile promises. His father, a veteran of the Great War, steadfastly believed that he was first and foremost a German, especially since they were Reformed Jews, only attending services on the High Holy Days and even attending a synagogue where the men and women could sit next to each other (this Judy couldn't imagine).

He told her that his father had been arrested on *Kristallnacht* on that terrible night in November of 1938, sent to a camp called Dachau, never to be seen or heard from again. He told her how his mother had committed suicide by swallowing a handful of sleeping pills a year later, never having recovered from the disappearance of his father. He told her how he and his sister Marta had agreed to split up after they were told they would have to leave their spacious house in Berlin's fashionable Mitte neighborhood, their home to be "repurposed" for high ranking party officials. They knew that if they were to move into the area of the city where Jews were being forced to live then, they stood a greater chance of being arrested and deported east. But that didn't stop Marta from being arrested for having fake papers and taken to the deportation center at the synagogue on Levetzow Street and subsequently sent east to the infamous Lodz ghetto, where she was never heard from again, just like their father. And he told her how when his own time came he was arrested on a particularly cold and snowy day in December 1943 and placed in a boxcar at the Grunewald freight yards that truly was only fit to transport cattle. He said the journey to Auschwitz was hellish and that had he known of the true hell that was to come once he arrived, he would have preferred to die during the journey, like some of the older people and children had.

Sam stopped talking then, his voice having become hoarse, ringed with emotion.

"It's okay, you don't have to tell me anymore," Judy told him, placing her hand on top of his to attempt to comfort him. She felt terrible for having caused this stranger so much pain, for making him relive these painful memories all so that her curiosity could be fed when all he had wanted to do was come to a dance and forget about it all.

He didn't say anything but instead twisted his hand and laced his fingers through hers. "Is it okay if I call you Yehudit?"

At that moment she would have agreed to anything to see this sad stranger smile once more. And so from that point forward he always called her Yehudit, the one person whom she didn't mind doing so.

In the beginning they kept their relationship a secret since good Orthodox girls didn't "date." Let alone go on dates with non-Orthodox Jewish boys their parents didn't know about. And even though he was technically Jewish, Judy knew her parents would feel that a Reformed German Jew was only one step away from her dating a *goy*.

So for the first couple of months they would go to dances that the Friendship Club or the Y was holding. Or at the Carnegie Library in Oakland where they would hold hands while they perused the stacks, always far away from the probing eyes of the librarian who sat at her desk appraising the patrons as if she were commander of a naval ship, about to chart her course into battle.

And once when they got caught in a freak storm, they dashed into the Cathedral of Learning, the tall imposing building that sat right on the University of Pittsburgh's campus.

"Before *Kristallnacht* I had always hoped that one day I'd be able to go to university, to continue learning," he told her, not looking at her as he said this but rather up at the massive arches that dwarfed the Cathedral's first floor. "You see after *Kristallnacht*, Jews were completely barred from attending any type of school in Germany."

They were sitting close together at one of the few empty tables, his hand holding hers, their fingers laced together, his right leg brushing hers when he would shift in the uncomfortable wooden chair.

"What did you want to study?" she asked him.

"Architecture."

It made perfect sense then, the way he could rattle off the names of the architectural styles of the buildings they passed, telling her this one was "neo-classical" and that one there was "Colonial Revival." Why just as they ran for cover from the deluge of water that was soaking them he had called out to her saying the Cathedral looked to be "Gothic revival."

"It's not too late you know," she told him. "You could still go back, get your degree. Besides how old are you?" She had realized then, just at that moment, that she had absolutely no idea how old the man she had been secretly seeing for the last two months really was. The problem with Sam and the other refugees she had met, friends of Sam's at the dances and other social activities, was that they looked older than their actual years, their bodies seemingly unable to recover from the horrific ravishing they had endured during years of brutal imprisonment. But it was the blank looks on many of the refugee faces that disturbed Judy the most, the looks that seemed to say, "my body is physically here, but I'm not. I'll never again be present among the living. I'm with my dead wife, my husband, my children, my parents, my brothers, my sisters back in Auschwitz, Sobibor, Treblinka, Mauthausen"-the names of the camps Judy had read about in the papers, where so many were murdered and even more gave up the desire to ever want to live again. Sam walked around with a perpetual air of sadness but his face still conveyed a look that said, "I survived, I live for the memory of all those who did not. I WANT to live." Judy was grateful for this.

He quietly laughed at this then, her not at all subtle but extremely blunt question, asking him how old he was. "How old do you think I am?"

Taking the question seriously while studying the face of the man she had grown to love being around the last couple of months, she answered, "30?" (she herself was 19).

He didn't say anything for a moment. He just looked intently at her. In fact the deafening silence made her worry she might have offended him with her guess. But then he gave her a small smile and said, "Pretty good guess. I'm 29. But it is too late. I'm much too old to return to school. My wanting to study to become an architect, that was from a former life, my old life," he reiterated. "Not to mention, everything was destroyed during the war. There's no record at all of my studies."

And with that he led her back outside where miraculously, the rain had stopped.

It was Sam who surprised her by saying he wanted to get her father's permission to marry her. She tried telling him that for Orthodox Jews, even Orthodox Jews in America, it didn't work like that. That in order for a girl to get married the *shadchan* first had to arrange a match that was approved by both of the families and since Sam had no family, not to mention he wasn't Orthodox, Judy didn't see how this could possibly work out. All he said to assuage her was, "Yehudit, just trust me."

And so she did or tried to as she anxiously waited for him to arrive at her family's house on Hobart Street early on a Tuesday evening. Her father, sitting in his favorite chair, was reading the latest issue of the *Jewish Daily Forward*. He much preferred that to the local Jewish newspapers *The Jewish Criterion* and *The American Jewish Outlook* since neither of those was published in Yiddish, her father's native language. Her mother was as usual not relaxing or sitting comfortably but rather hunched over on a little stool she had dragged over to one of the lamps in order to better see as she worked on her mending pile.

Her sisters Zipporah and Bina would no doubt scold their mother if they saw her straining her eyes as she was but Judy said nothing, knowing what it felt like to be nagged and pestered constantly by others.

Judy had thought about giving her parents advance warning about Sam's visit but had ultimately decided against it. What would it benefit telling them she had been secretly seeing a man who had no family, no rabbi who could vouch for him, who was not even a devout Jew, and worse, was a German Jew. (Her father had never liked the German Jews he had come across, feeling that they had always looked down on Jews like him, those from Eastern Europe who were generally more conservative, less educated, and poor.) She just hoped her father would at least let Sam say his piece (before throwing him out). She hadn't even considered what she would do once he was thrown out-would she leave, run away in the middle of the night to be with him? Would she stay, knowing she could never see him again, knowing that she would be forever restricted to the confines of the *eruv* and most likely never able to venture alone outdoors again? She pushed these thoughts from her head as a soft but determined knock sounded at the front door.

"Who could that be?" her father said in Yiddish, a slight look of annoyance passing across his face as he slowly rose from his chair to answer it.

Judy had wanted to get the door herself but knew her father didn't like when she did so, not to mention it would have looked pretty obvious she had been expecting Sam.

Her mother, unfazed, having more to do with the fact that she was unable to make out the words being spoken between her husband and this unexpected guest, continued her mending until her needle stopped in midair when she heard her husband gasp and then cry out her mother's name, "GOLDA!" Her mother gave Judy a startled look but then she dropped the shirt she had been mending in a heap at her feet and rushed off, adjusting her *sheitel* as she scurried from the room.

Her parents' heated voices, each of them attempting to speak over the other in Yiddish, carried into the front room where Judy still sat, unsure of what she should do. The good and obedient Judy knew she should remain here until her father called her (if he called her at all while Sam was still there). But the independent and free-thinking Judy, the American Judy as she considered herself to be, well that Judy wanted to go and stand by Sam, the man she loved. So that's what she did even as bile started to rise in the back of her throat.

Three sets of eyes fixated on Judy as she appeared, one set warm and encouraging, the other two confused and shocked over the blond-haired stranger standing in their home and what he had just told them.

Judy started to speak but her father cut her off, holding up his hand indicating he wanted to say something. He took a moment to collect his thoughts then began. "Judy, when you were little and got the polio, we thanked God that he spared you, our little *bubbeleh*," her father's voice breaking as he said this last word, a Yiddish term of endearment meaning little doll. "But then your leg was deformed and any chances of you ever finding a good match were completely ruined. But now this stranger here, who's not even from the community, who we know nothing about, says he wants to marry you, wants you to become his wife."

He paused then, going over to stand by Judy's mother, taking her hand in his. This sight astounded Judy for her parents rarely demonstrated any sort of affection in front of others, let alone in front of a stranger.

"My first thought was to throw this *meshuggener* out, how dare someone come into my home and say he wants to marry my daughter. And he's not even a good Jew, no *payois*, no *kippah*, nothing," referring to the sidelocks and skullcap that her father and all Orthodox Jewish men wore. "But he's a Jew. He's a Jew that survived when so many of our people did not. He survived just like you did during that awful summer when you got the polio, when the doctors said you probably wouldn't live and when so many children died. God wanted you two to meet, for you are both survivors of immense strength and resilience."

And then the words Judy had only dreamt her father would say, never actually imagining he would-"And I will never stand in the way of a union that God has clearly preordained. You have my permission to marry."

They were married on a blustery, cold day in early December 1951 at the Tree of Life Synagogue, the conservative *shul* Sam had been attending since he had come to Pittsburgh with Rabbi Hailperin officiating. Although he had been willing to shed his "reformist roots" as her father referred to Sam's religious upbringing (or lack of it) back in Germany, he had told her privately he could never belong to a branch of Judaism that still carried on like it was the 17th century, and most especially not in a place like America.

But Sam's willingness to become a Conservative Jew at least, someone who wore a *kippah* all the time now, and once a week came to her house to study the Talmud with her father, was enough to mollify her parents. He was also becoming quite adept in Yiddish, although it helped that German was so similar to it.

As Judy watched her parents doing the *Mizink*, the dance for the parents of the bride when their last child is wed, Judy gave a silent prayer of thanks to God for having brought this German Jewish refugee into her life and making all of this possible, to let her become Mrs. Samuel Weiss.

✤ CHAPTER 3 ✤

Pittsburgh
March 2002

"Dad?" Becky called out as she unlocked the front door to her parents' house. She still called it that, her "parents' house," even though her mom had been dead for nearly five years now. But every time she stepped inside the 1930s duplex she swore she could still smell the scent of her mother's perfume (Joy by Jean Patou, the only fragrance she ever wore, the only feminine luxury she ever allowed herself) wafting through the air, the faint aroma of *bubbe's* recipe for homemade chicken noodle soup beckoning from the kitchen as if it were simmering in a pot on the stove there and not just in her imagination.

"God damned hypocrites!" her father cried out as Becky stood in the doorway of the living room where her father sat perched upright in his recliner (not at all reclining), his eyes transfixed to the small television set before him.

"Dad, what on earth is the matter?" Becky asked, not wanting her visit to start like this, her father upset. She felt terrible in thinking it but she truly hated coming here, coming to this house anymore with her mom not there. She and her father had never really gotten along but when her mom was alive, she had been able to serve as the buffer, the peace mediator between them. With her gone, there was no one to soothe her father's moods, his outbursts, his overall discontent with the world, and Becky had absolutely no desire to fill those shoes.

She of course did her daughterly duty by stopping by once a week for a visit, making the short drive from her apartment in Bloomfield to Squirrel Hill, unloading the groceries she had brought him, making one or two meals for the week that he could just heat up, attempting to have a conversation that didn't divert into a full-blown rant about something (always on his part, mind you). And she always answered his calls even if his penchant for middle of the night telephoning majorly irritated her.

"God damned hypocrites," he repeated, using the television remote to point at the screen where a morning news program was being aired.

"Yes, you said that already," Becky replied, a bit exasperatedly.

"These Arabs," he said disgustedly, "they won't stop until every last Jew is dead. They're just like the Germans."

Becky watched as the muted TV showed a scrolling headline with the words "Passover massacre…30 dead…suicide bombing at the Park Hotel in Netanya…Hamas claims responsibility…deadliest attack against the Israeli people since the Second Intifada began."

"Our people are dying every day at the hands of the Palestinians, no bus, no café, no street safe," her father said, his voice becoming distraught. "And yet the world does nothing, the great America does NOTHING. The American people are so sympathetic to the cause of the Palestinian people but where were they when we German Jews tried to get visas after Hitler and his thugs came to power in the 30s? After the events of *Kristallnacht* when my father was killed? Where were they when they effectively sent hundreds to their deaths by refusing to let those passengers disembark here?"

For once, Becky couldn't disagree with her father, not about America's horrific isolationist policy in the 1930s, nor the tragic tale of the doomed voyage of the MS St. Louis. She remembered the first time she heard about the ship that in 1939 carried 901 Jewish refugees from Nazi Germany across the Atlantic, who were hoping to escape persecution, hoping to just straight-up survive. And how not one, not two, but three nations all denied the ship permission to land, thus forcing it to return to Europe, the people on board knowing that death most certainly awaited them. Various European countries took in the refugees but it was only a matter of time before those countries too were invaded by the Nazis and those same people rounded-up and deported to camps in the East from their adopted homelands. And these were Jews who all could have been saved.

"It doesn't help matters any getting upset about it. It's not good for your blood pressure," she told him.

"I've always wondered something," her father said. "Had you been alive in the 30s, I wonder if you would have tried to save the German Jews like you did the Soviet Jews."

Her father was referring to protests she had taken part in during the 1970s for the release of the Soviet Jews, the most infamous one being in 1975 at the Old Syria Mosque in Oakland when she had almost gotten arrested, a fact she had never told her parents.

"Of course I would have," she quickly replied and then, wanting to change the subject, asked, "so what do you want for dinner tonight?"

It was a 4th grade school assignment that had led Becky to ask her mom about her heritage, about where she came from. Judy had gotten out an atlas, showing her on the map roughly where Suwalk was, where Lithuania was even though the map read "Union of Soviet

Socialist Republics" to where she was pointing. She told Becky how her parents and brother and sisters had come to America, arriving in Pittsburgh in 1924.

"But what about Daddy?" Becky asked her.

Judy pursed her lips together, taking a moment before she continued. "Your papa is from here, from Germany," she said, pointing to Germany on the map's page.

"Which Germany?" Becky asked, peering closer at the page to see that there was not one but two Germanys listed.

"Oh, East Germany," she said. "The German Democratic Republic but when your papa was growing up, there was just one Germany," she added, almost as an afterthought.

"Is that where my other *zayde* and *bubbe* live?" Becky asked, thinking how cool it would be to go to another country.

"No my darling," her mother began. Taking Becky onto her lap she said, "Your other *zayde* and *bubbe,* papa's parents, they died a long time ago, during the war. You know about World War II, right? When all the world was fighting each other? You've started to learn about it in school, yes?"

"But why were they fighting?" Becky asked, still unable to understand how all the world could be so mad at each other.

"Because there was a very bad man who wanted to do very bad things and many people didn't like this so they tried to stop him."

To Becky at the time, her mother's explanation sounded like something out of a comic book. But that's the only explanation Judy ever offered to her about what had happened to her father's parents during World War II. It was not until 1967 when she read *Night,* Elie Wiesel's memoir about his experiences as a Jewish prisoner in the Auschwitz and Buchenwald camps and then the following year during the months of the trial of Adolf Eichmann, one of the architects behind the Final Solution, the Nazis' plan to exterminate the Jews of Europe, did Becky finally learn who this "very bad man" truly was. It wasn't until those two occurrences did Becky understand the enormity of the Holocaust, understand that series of numbers her father had on his arm, understand what her father had gone through as a young man.

It was on Becky's 13ᵗʰ birthday, when had she been born a boy she would have celebrated her *bar mitzvah*, that her father finally told her the story of his life, that is the life he had back in Germany before it was reduced to ashes in 1945.

While her mom and *bubbe* were at home, hard at work on her birthday dinner (her *bubbe* was living with them by that point after her *zayde* had passed), her father told her to get her shoes on, that he was going to take her for a ride.

When he parked in front of the Temple Rodef Shalom on Fifth Avenue, one of Pittsburgh's grandest and biggest synagogues, Becky said in a very teenager way, "So you're taking me to a synagogue?"

"Just come inside," her father replied in a tone brokering no further discussion.

Sighing heavily, Becky dutifully followed her father inside the grandiose building that fit in beautifully with the street that just further down was known as Millionaire's Row, where the rich and powerful of Pittsburgh society had built their homes less than a century before.

They sat in silence for a couple of minutes in a row at the back of the *shul*. "I like this synagogue because it reminds me of the one I attended as a child and young man back in Berlin," he began quietly. "*Neue Synagoge,*" he said in German, slightly startling her since he never spoke in his mother tongue.

"New Synagogue," parroting back, only in English.

"Yes, that's right. I wish you could have seen it," he said, his tone full of longing, was it? Nostalgia for the past? "It truly was one of Germany's finest buildings, the most beautiful synagogue you've ever seen, the best in all of Berlin. Of course the architecture was Moorish Revival, completely different from here which is Beaux-Arts," he added seriously, as if she were to be quizzed later on the architectural styles of different synagogues.

Becky wished her father would get to the point as to why he'd brought her here to a synagogue and on her birthday no less.

"I never wanted to speak about the past, about what happened to me in Germany and in the camps during the war. But your mother tells me you are no child anymore, that you deserve to know," he said wearily. "For Jewish boys, when they turn 13, they are considered an adult in our faith. Today you turn 13 and so I am considering you an adult, an adult who is mature enough to understand what I and our people went through."

His story began when he told her the names of her other grandparents and the name of his sister, a woman who would have been known as *Tante* Marta had she lived.

He described to her what they looked like, how his father, Benjamin Weiss, sported a thin mustache and had a scar that ran across the top of his left hand, a permanent legacy of his time as a soldier in the German Army during the Great War, along with his prematurely gray hair. His mother, Giselle, was a beautiful woman, the daughter of a rich banking family from Frankfurt who had wonderfully soft chestnut colored hair that she always wore in a perfect coif at the nape of her neck. She loved music (she had been trained as a concert pianist) and was always hosting dinner parties and other soirees at their elegant house in Berlin's Mitte district. And his sister Marta, she was younger than him by two years, but they were inseparable, "thick as thieves" was how their old housekeeper Katja described them as children. He

25

told her how her *Tante* Marta was fluent in four languages and had hoped to study French literature at university before the Nazis banned Jews from attending school. He told her that Marta was the spitting image of his mother, the two of them often being mistaken for sisters for how youthful Giselle looked.

"My family," he started, "we weren't very religious Jews, if you could even call us Jews. We would only attend shul on the High Holy Days. But once the Nazis came to power and could get away with anything, well, we stopped going to the *Neue Synagoge* altogether. My mother, she had Katja remove all traces of Jewishness from the house, putting them away in the attic lest a visitor see them and discover we were Jews."

"What happened to them?" she tentatively asked, still in disbelief that the man sitting next to her, the man who had never shown his emotions to others as he considered it a sign of weakness and vulnerability, was actually her father.

"They were all taken from me, one after the next. First my father, then my mother, then Marta, until finally it was just me, the Weiss family of Berlin who lived on *Kroenstraße* no more," and with that he started to cry.

Becky, who had never once been comforted by her father, comforted him that day, in the second to last row of the empty synagogue, on what was her 13ᵗʰ birthday.

Becky supposed there were two events that had caused the permanent strain in her relationship with her father. The first was her decision to major in social work, a decision her father had been vehemently against.

"Why would you want to study such a useless field?" he asked scornfully.

Judy winced at the derisive tone of her husband's voice, hating that he was making a scene in front of their company.

Even though it wasn't *shabbat*, Becky's mom had invited her sisters and brother and their spouses for dinner to celebrate Becky's admittance and full scholarship to the University of Pittsburgh. She had even surprised her with a chocolate chip chiffon cake from Waldorf's, Becky's favorite.

Becky hadn't mentioned her academic plans to anyone but her mom, who was in full support of them since she herself had wanted to be a social worker when she was her daughter's age. Becky had always loved the stories her mom used to tell her about the days when she volunteered at the Irene Kauffman Settlement, helping those new immigrants to Pittsburgh settle in, readying them for their new lives in the *Goldene Medina,* the promised land the Jewish immigrants to America imagined it to be. When her Uncle Moshe asked what she planned to study, naturally she told the truth, as she never expected her father to speak with such vitrol regarding the social work field.

"What's wrong with social work?" she answered back, her tone indicating that she was spoiling for a fight.

"Darling," her mom interjected, placing her hand on Becky's arm, "I don't think this - "

"When I came to this country," her father interrupted her mom, not letting her continue, "the social workers were supposed to help us survivors, make us feel welcome here. But you know something? They didn't even call us survivors, we were just a new group of greeners or immigrants or refugees to them. As if what we had gone through and endured was the same as every other Jewish immigrant who had come to America before. I never felt welcome a damn day here until I met your mother at that dance the Friendship Club was hosting," he said.

Was her *bubbe* staring at her father because of his outburst, Becky wondered? Or that he had said the word "damn?" She found it funny that even after all these years in America, her *bubbe* would still be shocked to hear a word as relatively innocent as damn being uttered.

"We arrived in America having lost everything. All of our families were dead, we had no one, no one to comfort us, to talk about what we had been through, about the hell we had endured for years in the camps. They just didn't care, they never asked how we were doing, and yet they made us each week go to the Jewish Social Service Bureau for review." He said the word "review" with utter disdain. "We were told to 'move on,' like it was just as easy as snapping one's fingers. And thank goodness I knew English, thanks to my father. I knew so many refugees who only spoke Yiddish or Polish and those worthless social workers were even more worthless then. And another thing, where did the American-born Jews get off being embarrassed by 'us'? The world's always hated Jews, it doesn't matter where we relocated to. The world's always wanted us **dead**."

The room had fallen silent during her father's tirade. And when he was finally finished, it stayed silent until her *bubbe* said, "cake"?

The second event was when Becky announced she would be marrying Danny, her non-Jewish boyfriend, which made the whole majoring in social work issue seem innocent in comparison to how he reacted to news of her engagement.

She had met Danny at Pitt, when they were both freshmen. He was also from Pittsburgh, having grown up in the city's Polish Hill neighborhood. A second generation American, his grandparents had emigrated from Poland in the early 1900s.

Becky had never really dated anyone before Danny, although it wasn't from lack of trying on her part. Although she was forbidden from going out with boys in high school, there had still been plenty of necking and even a couple of times where she had allowed the boy to go to second base with her. But these instances always happened in secret, usually in the front seat of the boy's car or in the back of the auditorium at Taylor Allderdice High School. The one and only time she had tried going to the movies with a boy, two hours of carefree necking and holding hands, she had apparently been seen entering the theater with Mickey Kenny, her fingers laced with his, by none other than Mrs. Lilenblum, Squirrel Hill's very own Jewish Hedda Hopper. By the time she returned home, Mickey having dropped her off two blocks away from her house, her parents had already been given the full report of her shameful activity with the "red headed *goy*." After that, she wasn't allowed to go to the movies for three months and even once her punishment was done, she could only go with her mom, who thankfully liked seeing pictures (unlike her dad, who never went).

She and Danny had both been in Professor Addington's Western Civilization class, a pre-requisite for all freshmen, which met on Tuesday and Thursday mornings. Becky was someone who always arrived to her classes on time, a regimen that Danny did not follow. So when he arrived to class a minute late, thus being greeted with a stern and disdainful look from the septuagenarian professor, Danny paid him no mind, instead just sliding into the lone empty seat next to Becky's in the first row.

When he nudged her with his elbow a few moments later, pretending to write, his eyebrow raised in a question that he was in need of a pen, it was only then that Becky took a good look at the boy sitting next to her. He was tall with dark features but had the bluest eyes she had ever seen on a person. They stood in stark contrast to the tan color of his skin. When she handed him a pen from her satchel, he smiled at her in thanks before returning his attention to the myriad of scribbled lines of text and dates that the professor had managed to add to the chalkboard in only seven minutes of class so far.

At the end of class, the boy with the dark hair had rushed out before Becky could ask for her pen back. Collecting her things, she left the classroom only to hear someone say, "Thanks for the pen." And there he was, her tardy seatmate, leaning casually against the wall, a few feet away, holding up her pen as if in question.

"I thought you had left," she said, hoping she sounded as casual as he looked as she walked towards him.

"I wanted to get out before the professor could castigate me for my tardiness," he told her sarcastically.

"Danny," he said, holding out his hand to hers.

"Becky," she replied, her heart starting to beat a little faster.

"Nice to meet you Becky, want to grab a hot dog?"

And it was on her first unofficial date with Danny that Becky had her first hot dog, well a non-kosher one. When she took her initial bite of that forbidden food it was then and only then that Becky thought she would be going to hell sooner rather than later. That it was a sin much more egregious than any other prior ones she had committed, even the time she necked with a Gentile on *Yom Ha'atzmaut*, which marked the founding of the state of Israel. But it tasted so good she thought as she hungrily devoured it, her father and the *halakha*, the Jewish law which dictated so much of her daily life, soon forgotten.

They started going steady after that, since now she could go out with any boy she wanted to as a couple of miles separated her from her father and the Mrs. Lilenblums of the world.

It wasn't just his good looks that drew Becky to Danny. It was that he was genuinely interested in what she had to say, her thoughts as a female in 1970s America, when the topic of feminism was truly starting to make waves. Having grown up in a household but also a culture where a woman's voice was expected to be silent, it was so refreshing to be with someone of the opposite sex who actually wanted to hear her speak. He even told her once that he was glad she wasn't like all the other girls at Pitt, girls who were "only interested in getting their MRS degree." Becky, unsure of what a MRS degree was, looked at him blankly, waiting for an explanation.

"You know, a girl who just wants to become a MRS, find her perfect husband, have 2.5 children," he said." I want to get married, don't get me wrong but…," his voice sounding sheepish, trailing off then. "But I want my wife to always be herself too, to not give up who she was or what she loved just because she became a Mrs."

Becky knew then at the age of 18 that Danny was the man for her. She knew that he would never ask her to give up her studies for a life of domesticity with him, to forgo any aspirations she had of becoming a working woman all so she could have dinner on the table for him each night. But she also knew that her staunch and conservative and stubborn Jewish father would never accept a boy in her life who wasn't Jewish.

Becky met Danny's family shortly before the end of their freshman year. He had invited her to come to Sunday dinner, which really was lunch in the Kowalczyk house but a huge affair all the same. After Mass at nearby Immaculate Heart of Mary (which thankfully he had not invited her to), Danny's mom and two sisters plus his two brothers' wives all set to work in the kitchen preparing a massive meal, under the watchful eye of his *babcia,* his grandmother. He said that it was a Sunday ritual more or less.

Even though all of Danny's family was tan and dark like him, for the first time in her life Becky was glad she had gotten her father's fair looks-his dark blond hair and pale skin, a stark contrast from her mom's thick dark hair and bushy eyebrows.

It nagged at her but in all the months they had spent together, she still hadn't told him she was Jewish and still wasn't sure if he would care or not. Although her last name of Weiss was typically a Jewish surname, it was also a German one and meant "white" in both Yiddish and German. But Becky hoped that to his family, a group of strangers who didn't know her or anything about her and her family, she could just pass as being German for once.

Later that day she couldn't remember all the names of the foods passed around the large table during the meal except for the pierogi, the little potato and cheese dumplings, and *bigos,* a type of meat stew his *babcia* explained in broken English, "Keep you warm on cold Polish night when you no have man next to you," which made everyone laugh except for Danny's mother, who said, "*mamusia!*" in a scolding tone.

The dinner had gone well, Danny telling her the next day before class that everyone had really liked her, adding that his *babcia* said she was very pretty. So as she expected and feared would happen, it wasn't too long after that he started asking her when he could meet her parents.

For a couple of weeks she made excuses, saying her *bubbe* was unwell and that her mom was tending to her 'round the clock. And then she said her father was busy with work, having to stay late most nights at the office (neither was in fact the truth). He accepted the lies at first but then grew frustrated, feeling like there was something she wasn't telling him.

"Do they not know about me?" he asked angrily, stopping dead in Schenley Park where they had been walking.

Not wanting to lie anymore and before she could stop herself, Becky blurted out, "I'm Jewish."

He didn't say anything for a moment but then he leaned his head back and started laughing.

"Why's that funny?" she asked semi-defensively.

"Because you honestly thought that would bother me? I knew you weren't Catholic which is why I didn't ask you to go to Mass. I just thought you were Protestant. I never would have guessed Jewish, but so what?"

"You don't understand," she began. "My father, he's very strict, very conservative. He doesn't like *goyim*." At his blank look she added, "non-Jewish boys."

"He'll like me," he said in that very cocky, very Danny way of his which normally she found endearing but today, now, she just found annoying, his not understanding what she was saying.

"He's a Holocaust survivor."

"Was he in the camps?" Danny asked, asking with the same type of almost morbid curiosity others had before him when they learned her father had survived the Holocaust.

"Yes, but look, it's not just that," she began, preferring not to elaborate anymore on the subject. "He doesn't like, doesn't trust non-Jews. My entire life, he never has," she said flatly.

"It's 1974, not 1933. I'm a good guy, please give me the chance to show your father that."

And so she did. They made plans for Danny to come to her house one afternoon in much the same way 20 years before Judy and Sam had so he could come and meet her ultra-Orthodox parents. The glaring difference was not that Becky wasn't considered "marriageable," but rather that no man would ever be good enough for Samuel Weiss' Rivkah, let alone a *goy*.

Besides the fact that he wasn't Jewish and that he was also Polish ("the Poles were just as bad as the Nazis during the war, collaborator scum they were," her father had said on many occasions), Danny was also pre-law, the career path SHE was supposed to have taken. As a child, her father liked to tell friends that "Rivka" was going to be the next Cecilia Goetz, the only American female prosecutor at the Nuremberg Trials and who was also a Jew, the most important part. She knew that Danny's studying to become a lawyer while she was not would only fuel her father's dislike of him even more.

The sound of the doorbell ringing at the designated time made Becky jump up from the chair she was sitting on in the living room but then she had to make herself walk normally to answer the door so as not to arouse suspicion on her part. Her mom was watching old re-runs of "Bonanza" (her favorite television program for whatever bizarre reason; Becky had never understood this) while her dad read the *Post-Gazette* in his preferred chair. She opened the door to find Danny grinning broadly at her, taking her hand in his and squeezing it in support and encouragement she supposed.

When they stood in the entrance of the living room, Becky watched her dad lower his paper, all the while appraising the young man who stood before him. No one had said a word but Becky could already see her dad's features harden, his blue eyes seeming to become the color of steel.

"Mom, dad, I'd like you to meet Daniel Kowalczyk," Becky said. Then after a pause she added, "my boyfriend. Danny, this is my father, Samuel Weiss and my mother, Yehudit Weiss."

Becky wondered which had angered her father more-hearing Danny's last name spoken (he had a knack for languages and would have immediately known it was Polish, unlike most Americans who would politely ask, "now where's that from?") or her saying the word, "boyfriend." In both instances, she had seen her father's nostrils significantly flare up. She knew her mother would have seen this too, even if Danny had not.

"Very pleased to meet you, sir," Danny said, advancing towards her father, outstretching his hand to shake. When Sam still had not risen from the chair he was sitting in, clearly ignoring the proffered hand before him, Danny finally lowered his, taking a step or two back as if in retreat.

Becky felt sick to her stomach and only a couple of moments had passed since the doorbell rang.

"Shall I put a pot of coffee on?" Becky's mom asked, always the diplomat. "I just made some fresh *rugelach* earlier today."

"That would be lovely Mrs. We-"

"That won't be necessary Yehudit," her father said, cutting Danny off mid-sentence. Rising from the chair as he spoke he continued, "Mr. Kowalczyk, I'm afraid this isn't a very good time for my family. My wife's mother has been ill as of late and I have an early day tomorrow. If you'll please take your leave now, we'd be most grateful for your understanding."

Becky stood rooted to where she had been standing, still not speaking even as her father was essentially throwing her boyfriend out when all he had done was wanting to meet her parents.

Danny didn't speak but clearly was begging her to speak up, to say something, anything, from the imploring look he was giving her with his eyes. When she remained motionless, he took one last look at her, disappointment and even hurt now visible across his usually carefree and happy face.

"I'm sorry to have bothered you, Mr. and Mrs. Weiss. Goodnight," he said stiffly, the sound of the door closing behind him echoing in the otherwise silent house.

Her father told her she was forbidden from ever seeing that *goy* again. He had hated Danny. There was no getting around it. No amount of Danny's persistent warm personality or charisma could change Samuel Weiss' opinion of him, not that he had really given Danny any chance to show it.

When she yelled back at him saying he couldn't stop her, that she was in love with Danny, Sam said in such a cold tone even for him, "I will disown you and throw you out of the house if you do." At this her mom finally stood up, crying out "enough" which startled all three of them as Judy wasn't prone to ever raising her voice.

When her mom's light knock on her bedroom door came hours later, Becky wasn't sure how the conversation would go. Yehudit Weiss wasn't one to ever go against the wishes of her husband, but nor was she going to lose her only child, especially when she herself had initially disobeyed the wishes of her parents and gone against the path of her religion. She told Becky, "I threatened your father with a Jewish divorce if he continued with his threat. That stopped him cold." A slight mischievous glint shone in her eyes as she said this.

So Becky was "allowed" to still see Danny, she just was never allowed to bring him to her house or mention him in front of her father. It wasn't the greatest arrangement since Danny still lived at home in a house with five other people but they made it work until he became increasingly frustrated with their lack of privacy, their lack of ever having any time alone. So when he asked her to marry him in their junior year of college she didn't think twice before accepting, wanting so desperately to move out of her father's house and to truly start her life with Danny.

As neither was willing to convert to the other's religion, they were married in a civil service at the courthouse. All of his family were there but she had overheard multiple members of his family saying "it's not a real marriage." But at least they came. Only Becky's mom and her *bubbe*, who had become quite liberal in her waning years, were there for her.

And for the entire time that Becky and Danny were married, her father refused to acknowledge it, Danny still forbidden from going to her parents' house, something her mom couldn't ever get her father to budge on.

But it wasn't until Becky arrived at their house one unseasonably warm fall afternoon 12 years later, her mascara running, her eyes bloodshot from all the crying she had already done, that she said in a mangled voice, "Danny wants a divorce, he says he's met someone else."

It was then that her father finally acknowledged it by saying, "I told you that you shouldn't have ever married that *goy*."

CHAPTER 4

Pittsburgh, Pennsylvania

She hadn't breathed a word of it to anyone but it taken years for Becky to save up enough money for her trip to Germany. The salary she earned working as a social worker at Montefiore Hospital basically meant she would never know a day in her life what it felt like to be rich. And that was okay. The money aspect of the job had never really bothered her, she hadn't become a social worker for that. Rather, she had defied her father all those years ago and entered the field to help those who needed help the most. Becky had wanted to be the type of advocate who genuinely wanted to help people, save them even, who didn't just look upon it as a job. She wanted to be there for people in the way the social workers had never been for her father and the other survivors after they had come here, instead looking upon them as a nuisance, indifferent to the trauma they had been through and the immense losses they had suffered.

Although she and Danny had talked about traveling, entertaining ideas of backpacking across Europe after they graduated, that had never happened. Money was extremely tight for them, especially after Danny started law school; her salary as a newly minted social worker was barely enough to cover their expenses. And then, once he had graduated from law school, there was always work. His dream of one day practicing his feeble French on the streets of Paris and enjoying a cappuccino against the backdrop of a Roman piazza had been replaced by his fervent desire to be the youngest attorney to make partner at Shimer and Solomon Law Firm.

After her divorce, any hopes and dreams Becky had about visiting Europe had seemed to be permanently tabled until the night of November 9, 1989, when she, along with thousands of other Americans, watched transfixed as NBC Nightly News host Tom Brokaw reported live from Berlin the night the Wall came down. Knowing that the Cold War was finally over, that the most oppressive symbol of Communism had been destroyed, now reduced to being just another historical fact in textbooks, ignited in Becky a strong desire to finally discover who she was, to learn where the German side in her came from.

As she watched the jubilant people of Berlin that night on camera, a mixture of both young and old, excitedly dancing and hugging, chipping away at this symbol of so much hate and oppression with their hammers and picks, Becky realized that any of those people she saw could have been her relatives, could have known her father when he was a young man, could have been neighbors to his family, classmates of her Aunt Marta. Becky didn't even know what part of Berlin her father's childhood home was in-whether East or West. But she wanted to know this and so much more. She wanted to see if the building on *Kronenstraße* still stood; if the grandiose *Neue Synagoge* where her father had once worshiped on the High Holy Days had been destroyed in the bombings during the war; and even to say goodbye to the aunt she had never met at the synagogue on Levetzowstraße, the site where she had been deported.

Pittsburgh, Pennsylvania
1990

"Mom, I'm not sure when I'll have enough to get there, but I'm going to Germany one day. I want to see where I come from."

Judy had looked at her daughter in slight surprise but then smiled at her. "Well, just don't tell your father your travel plans," she replied, more serious than joking.

Becky had invited her mom to the movies, a pastime the older woman still absolutely loved, and one in which she was never able to get her husband to share her enthusiasm. They had just seen the film *Europa Europa* which they had been discussing at length over a plate of grilled stickies at Eat n' Park.

"How I miss Weinstein's," her mother said longingly as she stroked the countertop of the booth they were sitting at, as if it were a fine white tablecloth and not made of Formica.

"The #10 especially," Becky replied, referring to the combo that included a hot corned beef with coleslaw and Russian dressing, brisket, pickles and chocolate cake.

"The fact that you as a little girl could eat all of that food by yourself never ceased to amaze me," her mom said as she smiled at her daughter.

"Dad always said I had to clean my plate. How long now has it been gone?"

"The fire was in '69. Murray and Beacon was never the same after Ben sold it," her mom said, almost with a trace of sadness.

"But Germany, do you think it's crazy me wanting to go?" Becky asked, wanting some reassurance since she doubted herself constantly ever since her divorce.

"Crazy, no, problematic because of your father and his feelings, yes," Judy said matter of factly. "But does that mean I wouldn't support you going there? Not at all my *bubbala*," she said putting her hand on top of Becky's. "More and more survivors are going back these days, going back to their hometowns, to the camps. I only wish your father would go. For closure, to finally bury those ghosts that have haunted him for all these years now."

And then her mom said something that Becky would always remember, would always make her wonder about even though when Becky brought it up years later Judy denied ever having said it, claiming Becky must have misunderstood.

"Your father and I have always shared everything, have always been the greatest of both partners and friends. But even after almost half a century together, I still feel there's something he's never told me, some deep dark secret he's always kept from me."

"What do you mean Mom? A secret? A secret about what?"

"There just have been times where I don't feel your father was who he said he was."

Pittsburgh, Pennsylvania
2005

It was only when Becky had started planning her trip, her bedtime reading now consisting of perusing the pages of a travel guidebook on Germany she had borrowed from the library, did she feel it was time to finally confront the label she had unwillingly been given ever since the day she was born-that she was the child of a Holocaust survivor.

Of course in a sense it was easy enough to forget this growing up, what with the subject being almost taboo in her house save for holidays and birthdays, birthdays of the dead, that is. It was on those days that Becky as an adult knew her father had been drinking, the uncontrollable sobs and strangled cries a combination of the alcohol and the sheer pain from remembering. She knew how much it had taken her father to share that little bit about his past with her on her 13th birthday and vowed then that she wouldn't ask him about the Holocaust after seeing how much pain it caused him to tell her those things.

But then on a cold day in November, a few days after Thanksgiving when Murray Avenue was bustling even more than usual with holiday weekend shoppers, she ran into Saul Abramoff, once a classmate of hers growing up, a rare fellow Yid at the predominantly WASP filled Colfax Elementary and Taylor Allderdice schools. They had lost touch after graduation when he went to Yeshiva College in New York and she stayed behind to attend Pitt.

"Rivka! I can't believe it, is it really you?"

Becky was stunned to see that the same boy she had known as a teenager who liked to slick his hair back to complement his daily attire of blue jeans and his prized black leather jacket now looked like a younger version of her father in a plain conservative black suit.

"Have you been talking to my father?" she jokingly asked, "as no one calls me that except him. But what about you? Where's the boy I used to know, is he still under there?" pointing to the *kippah* that rested atop his close-cropped, almost shorn hair.

"I became more devout at the Yeshiva, and then I met Gallina, She's-

His words cut off then until he said with the excitement of a small child, "Hey, I live in Israel now. It's much too cold to be standing around outside in this weather like *schmucks*. Let's grab a slice for old time's sake!"

Over slices of cheese pizza and pop at Mineo's, a beloved spot of theirs in their high school days, Saul filled her in on the last 20 years of his life. She feigned interest, not really wanting to hear at length how amazing Gallina, his Israeli-born wife was, or the fact that his twin girls, Yael and Shira, were geniuses as they each spoke five languages. It was only when he mentioned that he had traveled to Poland with his parents recently and visited Auschwitz, the infamous death camp and stuff of nightmares, did her interest pique.

"Wait," she said. "Your parents were in the camps?"

"Yes," he told her, taking another bite of his pizza. "That's where they met…at Auschwitz."

"When you were a kid growing up, did they talk to you about it? What they had been through during the war?"

"Oh gosh no. Are you kidding me? The only time my father ever hit me was when I asked my mother why I didn't have any grandparents or aunts and uncles and cousins. She broke out into sobs, I got cuffed," he said rubbing an imaginary spot above his temple as if it still hurt. "Lesson learned; I never brought it up again."

"But then what changed??" she asked, thinking she probably sounded more demanding than she should have.

Saul looked at her for a second then, his face revealing his surprise over the intensity of her tone but then said, "I started attending this group, for children of survivors."

So long after their pizza was gone, their cups of pop containing nothing but the remains of the melted ice, he told her how the group had helped him to look upon his parents as "whole people" and not just survivors, including the people they were before and during the war as well. Not just the people they became after the camps were liberated. He said the group had helped him to help his parents finally "complete" the mourning process, to leave behind the denial stage where they both had been stuck for half a century.

"Once I opened up to my parents, they finally after all this time opened up to me, the never-ending large amounts of both anger and guilt they had felt and kept within them for so long, internalizing their pain. Anger over what the Nazis had done to them, anger that their parents hadn't been strong enough or fought harder to stay alive, and then guilt over being the ones to survive when no one else did."

Wiping a stray tear from the corner of his eye he said, "Rivka, to be with my parents there, at that place, it made me feel for the first time in my life that I finally knew who they were."

"My dad was there," she said.

"Where?" he asked.

"At Auschwitz."

"What, he's visited too?"

"No, he was a prisoner there."

"Oh, I didn't know that. I knew he was from Germany, I just thought he had gotten out before the war. He always looked so healthy compared to my parents and some of their survivor friends I had met growing up."

Healthy, Becky thought to herself? Really? What was that supposed to mean? She had never really given much thought to her dad's physical appearance when she was a kid. The tattoo on his arm and the haunted look in his eyes were enough of a reminder about the hell he had been through. But there was some truth to what Saul said, thinking back and remembering what his parents had looked like. Mr. Abramoff had always looked incredibly gaunt to her and Mrs. Abramoff's skin had always had a pale yellowish pallor to it, while her father had always maintained a healthy, athletic build to accompany his golden hued skin. But how was that his fault? A survivor is a survivor.

"Well, I don't think it's really fair or even possible to say all survivors look the same," she said in response. "Everyone's story was different."

"No, I guess you're right."

They parted shortly after, promising to keep in touch, but Becky not planning to. She wasn't sure why, but Saul's comment about her father not looking like a survivor still miffed her, which she had no explanation for. Becky had never been one to champion her father before, ever in fact.

CHAPTER 5

Pittsburgh, Pennsylvania
2005

If there was one good thing to come out of her running into Saul Abramoff, it was that it inspired her into looking to find her own group for children of Holocaust survivors. She wasn't sure how much good it would do now, for her or her relationship with her father, seeing as how she was in her 40s, he now 84, both of them stubborn as mules. But maybe it was like Saul had said, that for many survivors, they had never moved beyond the "denial stage," thus contributing to the fractious relationship they had with their own children, since those children would never know who their parents had been BEFORE the war.

Becky inquired at the JCC and sure enough discovered that there was a group for children of Holocaust survivors that met the first Wednesday of each month. The woman told Becky that the group was called the "Second Generation," which Becky wasn't sure if she liked or not. How could she and other children of survivors like her who had been born in the safe confines of a world where Hitler and his Nazi monsters had been beaten, where they had been able to go to school and the movies, not fight for survival in the ghettos or wonder if they'd die tomorrow in the camps, be thought of as being anything like their parents? Becky had read enough about the Holocaust over the years to know she never would have survived what her father and others like him went through.

"You know, the woman who facilitates the Second Generation group, she also has one for survivors. That one meets the first Monday of each month," the woman from the JCC said on the other end of the phone, bringing Becky back to focus.

Becky didn't know what to say to this well-intentioned woman except to make up an elaborate lie and be glad that she had never bothered to change her name back after her divorce. "Oh, well thank you but my father has always been very open about his experiences during the war. In fact, he even goes to some of the local schools to speak with kids about it." Hitler could come back from the dead, the fate of the world depending on him, and Samuel Weiss still wouldn't sit in a room with strangers talking about what he had been through.

On the first Wednesday of the new month, Becky walked through the doors of Colfax Elementary, a place she hadn't stepped foot in for more than 30 years. It felt odd being back there but even more odd considering the reason why she was.

The woman who Becky assumed to be the facilitator looked to be a little older than her, smartly dressed in gray slacks and a black sweater. There were eight other people there, all around Becky's age, give or take, who all looked like her-comfortable and competent.

"Well, I see we have two new faces tonight," the facilitator said, warmly smiling in the direction of Becky and the man sitting next to her. "Welcome. My name is Sarah Feldman, Pittsburgh born and bred," to which the group softly laughed in response. "I'm a licensed therapist, I've facilitated Holocaust support groups for the last five years now as I had always felt there's a vital need for them. And I'm also the child of a Holocaust survivor."

Becky wasn't sure why but she hadn't ever thought that this facilitator would be someone like her. In her mind, she just hadn't lumped a children of Holocaust survivors group in the same category as those recovering from an addiction or surviving the loss of a child.

"Regardless of our personal experiences with our parents, we're all alike in the sense that we have all been pained by the suffering of the past," Sarah said. "We're all here because we're trying to understand our feelings of sadness, anger, anxiety that have unwillingly defined us for our entire lives. The bottom line is being a child of a survivor or survivors for some of you, is both a huge responsibility but also an overwhelming burden. I'm here, we're all here, to help us navigate this path we were put on by the sheer fact that our parents did not die in the ghettos or in the camps, but that they survived. They lived and from living they did not become just another statistic in the history books."

Sarah paused and then in a lighter tone said, "For the benefit of the newcomers, let's all go around the room and introduce ourselves starting with," pointing to the man sitting next to Becky.

"Hi, my name is Adam. My mom is a survivor. She was born in Kielce, in Poland." At the mention of Kielce, a woman sharply drew in her breath. "When she was 15, she was sent with her family, her parents, and her seven brothers and sisters to Starachowice Camp." He took a deep breath before continuing, his voice starting to break. "She and her two older sisters, they were immediately separated from their parents and her two older brothers. Her mom and her younger brothers and sister, they were sent to Belzec, a death center," he added. "She never learned the truth about her dad but thinks he was shot in the Piaski ravine. In 1943, there was an uprising at the camp. After the war, friends of my mom said that her two older brothers had been killed in it. When the camp was liquidated, my mom and her two sisters were sent to Auschwitz. They miraculously survived the rest of the war then, living to see liberation. They, they-"his voice broke off then, he took a moment before continuing. "They returned to Kielce after the war, they had nowhere else to go even though their home had been taken by Poles after they were rounded up in '41. They lived with other Jews, other survivors, for they were all in the same boat, in this house in the center of town. And then there was the pogrom."

Becky was stunned, unsure she had heard this Adam correctly. She knew all about pogroms from when her grandparents had talked of the old country, of life in the Pale of Settlement under the harsh and unjust rule of Tsar Alexander III and then his son, Nicholas II. But pogroms in Poland, AFTER the war?

"My mom's two sisters, they were both murdered by the Poles on that horrible day in '46. They had endured so much, been tested by God time and time again, only to be murdered by their fellow countrymen a year and a half after the end of the war," Adam said before starting to cry.

The group stayed silent, the only sound the box of tissues being passed towards Adam. When Becky handed it to him their fingers lightly touched, which Adam gave her a small smile of thanks.

"Growing up, my mom was never silent about her experiences during the war. She wanted my brother and me to know about what she had gone through, about the hell she had endured. About the unimaginable losses she had suffered, being the only survivor of her family, the only one to live out of a family of nine. But I never wanted to listen. She'd try to tell me it all and I'd just cover my ears. I was just a kid, I was born in this country, not back there. I'd get so mad at her thinking what was wrong with her to want to burden me with this, with tales of ravines full of dead bodies, of hunger in the ghettos, of death centers, of dead relatives who I would never know. I'm blessed because when I was old enough, no not old, but rather mature enough to listen, to finally really listen, I still had her around to tell me her story. She's also written everything down, every inconceivable hell she had gone through during the war so I'll never forget one detail. And what makes me the luckiest man in the world? I still have her in my life, she's still alive even at the age of 83."

He stopped talking then, looking at the people before him, something he hadn't done since he began almost as if for encouragement even though the hardest parts of what he said were behind him now. "And that will always be the greatest gift."

"Thank you for sharing your story Adam," Sarah said. "And now for our other newest member?"

"Well," Becky began, "I don't feel I have any right to talk after hearing Adam's story about his mom."

"We all have suffered," Sarah said firmly "Or we wouldn't be here."

"Absolutely," Adam said encouragingly.

"My name's Becky and my dad is a Holocaust survivor," Becky said. "He's German, was born in Berlin but I know so very little about his experiences. His dad was arrested after *Kristallnacht* and sent to a camp where he died, to Dachau. His mom committed suicide. And his sister, his only sibling, she was sent to the Lodz Ghetto where it's believed she died. He was sent to Auschwitz and survived to the end of the war there. He made his way back to Germany and lived in a displaced person's camp until he got the chance to come here." After a pause she added, "And that's about the extent of what I know of my dad's experience during the war."

"Is the little you know about your dad from what he's told you?" Sarah asked in a very professional way. "Or from what others have told you?"

"A little from my dad, more from my mom," Becky replied. "But still not much at all in the sense of actually knowing what he personally went through and experienced. I've read memoirs written by survivors and other historical references but it's just…it's just not the same."

"And you're right, it isn't," Sarah said. "There is no one single Holocaust story. They may have some of the same settings, the same evil villains, the same types of losses in the end, but no two survivors are alike."

Hours after the meeting had ended, Sarah's words, "no two survivors are alike" still struck a chord within Becky. She could read up on the Holocaust as much as she wanted. There was no shortage of Holocaust memoirs, now that half a century had passed since the end of the war. She wanted to read up on her own dad's experiences, to learn about the hellish journey that had taken him from Berlin to Poland, back to Germany during the couple of years he had spent in a displaced person's camp, to finally to America, to Pittsburgh, the place that had become his adopted home for nearly 50 years now.

Becky had liked the Second Generation group a lot. She planned to go back next month for another meeting because ever since her divorce and then her mom's death she hadn't felt like she belonged. She went to work and did her job because she had to. She went to her father's house twice a week, called him every day, because she felt obligated to. But the Second Generation group? This would be for her. And perhaps also a way to understand the complex and troubled man that was her father.

CHAPTER 6

For their tenth wedding anniversary, Samuel had surprised Judy with a weekend trip to New York City. He wasn't big on romantic gestures, never one to bring home a bouquet of roses or hold her hand when they were out, or even rub the small of her back when it was hurting (he was very Orthodox in that regard even if it was unintentional). And she didn't mind, not really. He was a good husband and a good father, even if she did find him to be too strict at times with Becky, considering she was just a child. He provided a good home, a good life for her and their daughter, and that's what mattered.

But when he told her about New York, she couldn't believe her ears, not even when he told her about the tickets he had gotten to see *How to Succeed in Business Without Really Trying*, since he hated the theater, especially musicals.

On their last night in the city before they would take the train back to Pittsburgh the next morning, he had taken her to a famous German restaurant in the East Village called Lüchow's. Judy was a little surprised by this since typically Sam wanted nothing to do with

German culture, especially food. She always remembered how, early on in their marriage, she had made *sauerbraten* for him, a traditional German roast, that a friend of hers from the Friendship Club had said was considered to be the national dish of Germany. Judy thought he would be happy to have a taste of home but it was the first time since she had known him where he had looked displeased with her. He ate his dinner, an uncomfortable silence present throughout the entire meal. But as she was clearing his plate, he quietly said, "I didn't come to this country to eat the food of the country that murdered my family. Please don't waste my money by making things like that again."

And she didn't. Which is why she was shocked to see him happily conversing away in rapid German with the waiter at this Lüchow's. When she watched him eat with such gusto from his plate, the same types of food he had derided her for making years before. She was perplexed, especially since none of it was kosher, and a lot of it was pork. But she knew better than to draw his ire when he clearly seemed happy and relaxed, rare form for him to be both at the same time.

When the massive indoor Christmas tree that stood only a few feet from them was lit, his eyes lit up like those of a child.

"They do this nightly," he almost yelled so as to make himself heard over the loud and chaotic noise of the restaurant's interior. "They start it around Thanksgiving and it goes till New Year's," he said. "The nightly lighting of the tree I mean."

"It's lovely," she yelled back, smiling at him.

"Did I ever tell you my family had a Christmas tree back in Berlin?"

"A Christmas tree?" she asked, somewhat puzzled.

"Yes," he said, taking her hand in his from across the table. "It was the best decorated Christmas tree on *Kronenstraße,* the best in all of Mitte in fact," he said emphatically, pounding his hand loudly on top of the white linen tablecloth as he spoke. Taking a sip from his massive stein he continued, "It was my mother's pride and joy at all the parties that she hosted each Christmas."

Judy knew her husband had grown up in a very relaxed Jewish household, nothing at all like her strict Orthodox upbringing. But the way he was speaking right now seemed almost as if he had been a Christian child back in Berlin, not the Jewish one he had actually been.

As he was helping her with her coat, Judy noticed a man curiously eyeing her husband as if he knew him.

Just then, this short, stocky man standing at the opposite end of the coat check area and who looked to be around Samuel's age asked in heavily accented English, "Don't I know you? Max, isn't it?"

All of the color had drained from her husband's face but in a sobering cold tone he said, "Excuse me, I think you have me mistaken for someone else. I've never seen you before in my life."

Ushering them to leave even though Judy hadn't yet finished buttoning her coat, the man called out, "Yes, that's it! From Berlin, from childhood! We were students at the *Berlinisches Gymnasium* together! I know I"-

The man's words were cut off then, lost to the noise of the Manhattan streets as the door of the restaurant closed shut behind them.

❧ CHAPTER 7 ❧

Germany
June 2006

"Sehr geehrte damen und herren, willkommen in München. Ladies and gentlemen, welcome to Munich," the pilot repeated, this time in English.

During the flight to Germany, Becky had pinched herself multiple times to make sure she wasn't dreaming, that her long awaited, long dreamt about trip was actually happening, that it was real. But this time, after hearing the pilot's message and looking out the window and seeing the Munich skyline before her, she had pinched herself the hardest and longest. And the small pink welt now on her left underarm was a visible reminder that all this was reality, her reality now.

Becky had chosen Munich for the sheer fact that it was a big city and she liked big cities. She appreciated them for their ability to offer people a little bit of everything but also because one never truly felt alone in them, even if you actually were. In big cities there were always enough people around, whether in stores or restaurants, where you didn't feel odd if you weren't walking with someone, or eating with someone. And that was the last thing Becky wanted to feel on her first trip to Europe. She simply wanted to enjoy every minute of it.

She had also picked Munich for its history. From the countless books she had borrowed from the library, she knew that the city was in many ways the origin story of the Nazi party, of Hitler's empire of evil. Heck, it was less than an hour away from Dachau, the first ever concentration camp, the place where her grandfather was thought to have died after being taken away during the night on *Kristallnacht*. The world knew the horrors of the Nazis and the events of the Holocaust during the years of World War II, but for the German Jews, the terror had started much earlier.

As she walked the streets she wished her mom could be with her right now. She knew the beauty of Munich's *plätze* was something Judy would loved to have seen, especially since each one had its own unique beauty and charm. She could just hear her saying, "Well, I really liked the *Odeonsplätz*, the Court Garden there IS lovely but can anything truly compete with the *Marienplätz*? I mean the people watching alone is worth spending a couple of euros each day on an overpriced coffee at one of those outdoor cafes with the surly waitresses."

After the collapse of the Soviet Union, they had talked about one day traveling to Lithuania together, to search out the village *bubbe* and *zayde* had come from all those years before when they left their *shtetl* behind to come to America.

Becky had visited the Holocaust Memorial Museum in Washington D.C. shortly after it opened, anxious to start a connection to her past, as tenuous as it was. She remembered being awestruck when she walked into the room called the "Tower of Faces," a three-story exhibit of 1500 photographs from a *shtetl* in what is today Lithuania, only to feel sickened and horrified when she read that the people of this village were massacred in two days of mass shootings during the war, a mere two days to wipe out an entire community. The photographs, the "tower of faces" was all that remained of this once vibrant community.

Becky never said this out loud but she often wondered if *bubbe* and *zayde's* village even still existed, if it and its Jewish residents had survived the death and destruction of the war years, or if the *shtetl* of her mother's people had just been another Ejszyszki, its Jewish people and customs wiped from the face of history.

"Wie viel?" Becky said in tentative German, pointing to the bouquets of vibrant yellow sunflowers. She had come to the city's *Viktualienmarkt* to start her day, eager to explore the famous market's many stands of culinary delights. She had already treated herself to three *brötchen* for her breakfast. She had gotten just one but then after discovering how good it tasted, she immediately went back for two more, saying to the stall keeper, *"zwei, bitte"* to which he heartily laughed and said in perfect English, "These are called *brötchen*, classic German breakfast rolls. Addicting, aren't they?"

"Incredibly so," instantly regretting talking with her mouth full. Her *bubbe* would have tsk-tsked at this had she been present and then said something along the lines that had Becky been born in my *shtetl* with manners like that, the *shadchan* would have said a cow would be her best prospect in terms of suitors.

"American?" the seller of the sunflowers asked.

"Yes, is it that obvious?" Becky replied with a smile.

"Not really," he said laughing. "If your German accent wasn't so bad, you easily could have passed for German or from one of the Nordic countries."

Becky felt her cheeks go red at the mention of her bad German accent. She had tried, even taking two semesters' worth of beginner German at the community college the previous year in preparation for her trip. But German pronunciation (unlike French, the language she had more or less been required by her father to take in high school) she found incredibly difficult.

"I'm actually German, well, half-German I mean. My father was born here, well, in Berlin I mean," she finished, knowing she was babbling inconsequential details about herself to a complete stranger who most likely could have cared less.

"Well, you definitely look the part," he told her. "Six euros for the flowers."

She eagerly handed him a 10 euro note, excited over the prospect of bringing these beautiful colored flowers to brighten up her otherwise dark and dismal hotel room that was near to the Isar Gate, one of the city's four main gates that dated back to the medieval era.

He handed her the now wrapped bouquet and turned his attention to a new customer who had been patiently waiting to be served this whole time but then added, "Enjoy the rest of the day *ziemlich amerikanisch*."

Becky knew what *amerikanisch* meant, the *ziemlich* part, well hopefully it wasn't anything too bad she thought as she began to meander once more through the stalls.

She had only been in Germany for two days and couldn't get over the kindness and helpfulness of the German people. Every person she had encountered so far and asked for help had been only too kind and eager to assist. She wondered, would their reception have been different had she inherited her mom's dark and in many ways, Jewish features. If she had not been born with blond hair and blue eyes would the people have looked at her differently? If she proudly wore the Star of David necklace her *bubbe* had given her on her graduation day from Pitt that normally sat in her mahogany jewelry box, would the people have eyed her suspiciously, wondering why someone "like her" was back here? She knew that these kinds of thoughts were ridiculous but she wondered, did every person of Jewish descent who had some personal connection to the Holocaust entertain this kind of thinking while being back in Europe. She wondered if Saul had thought this when he went to Poland.

Every time she saw or encountered a person around her dad's age, she couldn't help but wonder, "What side had this person been on during the war?" If they were a man, she wondered had they fought in it? Had they been in the SS, serving in one of the camps? Had they played a hand in the deaths of her grandfather or aunt? Had they been part of the reign of terror enforced at Auschwitz when her father had been a prisoner there? And if they were a woman, had they been one of those German women throwing flowers at *der Führer* like he was God at one of the infamous Nazi rallies and parades she had seen pictures of in books.

She couldn't help it but Becky found she liked the Germans. But was it wrong for her to do so considering what had happened to her people, to her own family, barely more than half a century before?

As she sat that night at dinner, hungrily eating her plate of *Nürnberger Bratwurst* and *sauerkraut* while taking small sips of her much too large stein of Augustiner Dunkel beer from time to time, she mused over how difficult tomorrow would be, the toll it would take on her emotionally still to be determined, for tomorrow she would be taking the S-Bahn, Germany's suburban rail, to Dachau concentration camp.

Becky had been amazed to discover that before it had become a camp, people had actually come to the town of Dachau for vacations, primarily to visit the Renaissance chateau and its other prettily painted 18th century buildings. She had just thought that all concentration camps had sprung up in desolate, barren places so the locals wouldn't see the terror taking place, not areas where people had come only a short time before for fun and frolicking.

Originally she hadn't planned on visiting Dachau. Becky hadn't wanted her entire trip to Germany, her first time anywhere really, to be solely tied to the tragic and incomprehensible events of the Holocaust because the fact was she still wanted to play the part of the carefree tourist. Not to mention, she didn't know when and if she'd ever be back, able to have enough money saved up again for a plane ticket to Europe.

Becky had wanted her time in Munich to consist totally of eating as much *spätzle* and *kartoffelklöße* as her stomach would allow (noodles and potato dumplings, two of her favorite foods) and checking off all the attractions her guidebook had recommended visiting. So far the *Residenz*, a incredible former royal palace right in the middle of the city, and the sweeping views offered from the top of *Peterskirche*, Munich's oldest parish church, had been her two favorite experiences. In both places she had pinched herself once more to make sure it had been real.

But then after one of her Second Generation meetings when she had been casually talking with some of the members, telling them of her plans for her upcoming trip, one of the men whose name she didn't know had bluntly asked, "Are you going to Dachau?"

"No, I hadn't planned to," she'd answered, not wanting to lie to the group but also not wanting to be derided for her decision to not visit, as if it made her a bad person, as if she didn't belong in this group of children of Holocaust survivors.

"You must," he'd said so emphatically that it annoyed Becky.

"You can't be a Jew, daughter of a German Jew no less, and not visit Dachau. Besides, it's so close to Munich you'd be foolish not to."

Becky didn't remind him that Dachau was where it was believed her grandfather had died. Then the derision would have really been laid on thick, she thought. Not wanting to prolong the conversation that had taken a decidedly awkward and painful turn she said to the group, "I need to head out everyone, still some work to review before court tomorrow." And then speaking directly to the abrasive and almost rude man she'd added, "I'll definitely consider it. Goodnight everyone."

So that night after the Second Generation meeting, as she had laid in bed looking up at the ceiling, she'd decided then and there she'd visit Dachau. Becky knew she owed it to the memory of her grandfather who had lost his life there and her grandmother who was never the same and had ended her own life when the love of her life was taken from her and sent there.

As Becky had walked up the path towards the camp only moments before, she periodically looked back and forth between the road and the gate she could see in the distance. On the second or third time of her doing this, an older man who looked to be a little younger than her father and who was walking with who she presumed to be his son said to her, "It's a ways back so they could hide what was really happening here, that it was a lot more than just a labor and re-education camp, the filthy lie the Nazis told the world. They constructed it like this on purpose."

"I see," Becky said, unsure if she could add anything of substance or intelligence to the conversation. Not knowing what else to say she asked, "Americans?"

"That's right, Alabama proud," he said, to which the young man he was with just smiled, almost embarrassed. "My older brother helped liberate the camp in 1945. He was with the Army's 45th Infantry Division. He died a couple of years ago but had always wanted to come back and see the place. So I decided to come for him and bring his son here," he said, indicating the younger man. "Tom Wallace," he said extending his hand to shake hers. "Becky Weiss," she said smiling, adding "And Pittsburgh proud.

"Jeff," the younger man said to her by way of greeting and then also extended his hand.

"History junkie?" Tom asked her as they continued walking. It was early in the morning on a weekday in early June and so the path was deserted.

"Um, not exactly," she replied, slightly stammering. Mentally debating if she should tell these strangers her personal history but then realizing that many people who visit the camps have some sort of personal connection to it, as this man and his nephew clearly did, she said, "My grandfather…he…he was a prisoner here. And died here, believed to have died here. There was never any grave or body."

"Damn," Tom said, Becky's statement clearly not what he had been expecting to hear. Jeff also looked taken aback but then tentatively said, "I don't know what to say in this instance; sorry doesn't exactly seem appropriate or fitting here."

"Oh, it's okay. I mean, it's not okay. It's just that, well, I obviously never knew him and it was so long ago but I knew I couldn't come to Germany and not pay my respects."

"Did you lose other family members?" Jeff asked, almost with morbid curiosity, something Becky had become accustomed to when people heard about her ties to the Holocaust.

"Jeffrey H.G. Wallace, it's none of your damn business," Tom scolded, his Southern drawl now coming in very thick and heavy.

"Oh, no, I don't mind, really," Becky said trying to assure the older man. "My father was the only one of his immediate family to survive the war. He survived Auschwitz and eventually made it to the States." The last part she said with a small smile, wanting them to know it was okay to have asked.

They were at the gate now and Becky looked up to see the words spread across it. *"Arbeit Macht Frei."* She had seen these same words in pictures of Auschwitz before, the cruel lie to make prisoners of the camps mistakenly believe that if they worked hard, they'd be set free. She wondered if her grandfather had been deceived by this lie when he had passed through this very gate himself 64 years before. She felt a chill thinking about this man, someone she had never met or knew what he had once looked like.

Knowing that she would want to be alone as she went through the camp and not tagging along with fellow Americans like she was on the streets of Munich's city center, she said to the men, hoping that she didn't come across as rude, "If you'll excuse me, I just need to experience this alone."

Tom and Jeff both started to speak at the same time but then Tom said, "Of course Miss Becky, we completely understand. I wish we could have met because of better circumstances but God bless you and your family, both the living and the dead."

Had he been wearing a hat, Becky would have sworn he would have tipped it at her just then, the beacon of Southern manners.

"Thank you," Becky said to Tom and then to both men added, "And thanks to the memory of your brother and dad for having liberated this place." Giving them one more smile she passed through the gate then, goose bumps appearing on her arm as she did so.

It was when Becky visited the Shunt Room and saw the personal possessions of the prisoners that she finally broke, streams of silent tears rolling down her cheeks.

It hadn't happened in Roll-Call Square where tens of thousands of prisoners, many of them exhausted and sick, were forced to stand, often for hours at a time, in the mornings and evenings, while they were counted or witnessed punishments. Or in the section of the camp called the bunker where apparently "special" prisoners were held, where torture and death was commonplace. And not even in the gas chamber where the most heinous of the Nazi crimes against the Jews were carried out.

No, it was in the room that reminded visitors to Dachau that every single person who had passed through the camp was once someone-someone's parent, someone's child, and someone's sibling. The pocket combs, the black and white photos of friends and relatives, the postcards written in haste by owners who never had a chance to mail them, were all tangible reminders of the lives taken.

❧ CHAPTER 8 ❧

Berlin, Germany
2006

Becky's train to Berlin had arrived late, getting into the city's Central Station (or *Hauptbahnhof*, a German word she didn't have the faintest idea how to pronounce), more than 90 minutes after its scheduled arrival time.

It's not that she'd had ambitious plans for her first night in Berlin but had hoped to see at least some of the capital city in the daylight. Instead the cab ride from Central Station to her hotel that was near Potsdamer Platz was completely in the dark. *C'est la vie* she thought to herself as tall darkened buildings whizzed by or *so ist das leben,* chiding herself then for not using the German phrases she had practiced so diligently before bed each night for nearly a year, including the phrase that meant, "that's life," a motto she needed to remind herself of quite often since her divorce.

When the clerk at the front desk of Becky's hotel pointed out various sites of interest on a paper map of Berlin, circling them in prominent red colored Sharpie marker, her ears perked up at the mention that the city's famous Holocaust memorial, the Memorial to the Murdered Jews of Europe, was less than a 10 minute walk away. All thoughts of tiredness and annoyance from her train's delayed arrival were completely forgotten when the clerk added that since it was an outdoor memorial it was open 24 hours a day.

So her first official day in Berlin wouldn't be a complete waste after all she thought, as she eagerly hurried off in the direction of the elevator.

"This is Germany's Holocaust memorial? This is how they chose to remember six million Jews the Nazis killed?" Becky said to herself almost out loud as she stared in disbelief at the thousands of vague and lifeless slabs before her.

Becky wasn't the biggest fan of abstract art but neither did she hate it. But this thing, this supposed memorial, it was just way too abstract for her, she thought, as she walked through its rows of nondescript slabs. How can something be called a Holocaust memorial when it was completely devoid of anything referencing or even tied to the Holocaust?

Becky thought back to all of the memorials she had seen at Dachau just the previous day, not that the whole of the camp itself wasn't a tragic but still beautiful living memorial. Especially upon hearing a bell ringing and learning from a tour guide who was standing at the ready, poised to answer any questions, that each day at 2:50PM, the bell rings to commemorate the exact time that the Dachau camp was surrendered to the 42nd Rainbow Division of the U.S. Seventh Army. Becky had looked around then for Tom and Jeff but hadn't seen them anywhere. She hoped they had heard the bell and would ask about its purpose, knowing how much it would most likely mean to them.

When she got to the one far end of the memorial, she saw a sign that read "*Ort der Information*/Place of Information." A pamphlet she picked up said that it "holds the names of approximately 3 million Jewish Holocaust victims, obtained from the Israeli museum Yad Vashem." Becky sighed to herself, feelings of annoyance returning over her late arrival into Berlin, as this was something she would like to have visited, wondering if there was a way to see if her grandparents' and aunt's names were among those included in the registry here or anywhere in Berlin for that matter. Were the names of Benjamin, Giselle, and Marta Weiss remembered by anyone other than her and her father, who had uttered them out loud to her only a few times her entire life? Did anyone know they had ever existed?

So ist das leben she repeated to herself as she turned back onto the darkened and almost eerily deserted *Ebertstraße* and started the short walk back to her hotel, not even realizing that the long since torn down Berlin Wall once ran along the length of the street she was currently traversing.

CHAPTER 9

Pittsburgh, Pennsylvania
1964

It was after her father's funeral that Judy started keeping a journal about Sam, specifically the things he had said and done that made her feel he wasn't really who he said he was.

This feeing, almost a suspicion, had nagged at her for years, intensified by the incident at Lüchows when she saw how stricken Sam had become over the stranger saying he had known her husband back in Berlin and then Sam's vehement and cold denial to the man's claim. Her suspicions finally came to a head the morning after her father died.

"You haven't packed your bag yet?" Judy asked coming into their bedroom.

"Bag?" Sam asked, his eyes trained on the mirror that rested atop her dresser as he adjusted his tie. "What bag?"

"Sam, really? You're as bad as Becky," Judy said with a tsk-tsk.

"I'd appreciate if you wouldn't compare me to a child as frivolous as Rivka," he replied in a cold tone. "For the last time, what is this bag you're talking about?"

Judy was stunned. In the 16 years she had known him he had

never once taken that kind of tone with her. He was now standing in front of her and when she finally raised her head to look up at him, hardened eyes the color of blue onyx were looking down at her.

"For *shiva*," she said tentatively. "We all stay with *mami.*"

"For how long?" he asked, clearly annoyed, his tone still not exhibiting an ounce of compassion.

"Seven days." Hoping she didn't sound condescending, for she knew how sensitive he became when it was occasionally pointed out he couldn't speak or read Hebrew, she added, "*Shiva* means seven in Hebrew. We mourn for a week, for seven days."

"So I'm supposed to work all day and then go to your mother's house when I'm done? Not have one moment to myself during these seven days?" he added, his tone giving way to anger that she could detect was just near to boiling over.

"Well, no. *Shiva* is just a time for mourning. There's no work, no school. People come to offer condolences." How could he not know this, Judy wondered?

He whirled back around at hearing this. "Seven days?" he yelled at her again, the veins bulging at his temples. "I can't take off for seven days to sit around your mother's house! I'll get fired!"

"Mr. Gumpertz is Jewish, of course he'll give you the time off," Judy said, hoping her words sounded calm and unruffled, thinking this would be the end of it. Naturally, it was not.

"Abe Gumpertz's family has been in this country since the 1860s! You really think a third generation American is going to give me seven days off so I can sit this *shiva* like we're living in some dirty *shtetl*?"

Judy wasn't one for getting mad at Sam. In fact she couldn't ever remember a time or situation when she had ever been...until now. And then said the first thing that popped into her head.

"Are you even Jewish?" she yelled back at him.

Sam froze, his face once again as pale and stricken as it had been that night at Lüchow's.

"I'll call Mr. Gumpertz now," he said quietly and left the room.

Of course Mr. Gumpertz had no problem with Sam being off for seven days so he could sit *shiva* with Judy and her family. Regardless of the type of Jew you were, you sat *shiva*.

The entire seven days at her mother's house he was polite and respectful to everyone and almost docile to her, a trait he had never once exhibited before.

The night after they returned home, Judy locked the door of the upstairs bathroom and took out the small black notebook she had purchased that day from Rosen Drugs and wrote-

> *Sam is not who he says he is. I just know it. There's something he's hiding, something he's not telling me. How could he do this to me, to our family?*

Pausing to wipe away the silent tears that had started to rain down her cheeks, she continued to write-

> *Is he even Jewish? Is his real name even Sam?*
> **<u>Who really is this man I married?</u>**

CHAPTER 10

Pittsburgh, Pennsylvania
1998

"What do you want?"

This was how Becky's father greeted her, now that her mom was dead. Now that there was no one to mildly scold him for his rudeness, his lack of manners, and his often overbearing demeanor. Judy had only been gone for three weeks but it might as well have been 30 years for how strained and emotionally draining the last three weeks had been. Becky hadn't only lost her mom, she had lost the one person, the only person probably, who saw some good in her father. But here they were.

"I told you on the phone the other night, I'm going through her stuff to get it ready to donate."

"And I told you, you little *meshuggener,* you're not touching or getting anything," he said, jabbing his finger in the air at her as he spoke.

Whirling around to face him on the steps, more than ready for a battle after the day she had had in which she had had to remove not one but two sets of kids from unstable homes, she yelled at him, "Then I'm done."

But they both knew her words were nothing but an empty threat. So she said the only thing that would pierce him, "She would be ashamed of you." And with that she continued to go upstairs. And heard nothing more from him.

"What's this?" Becky quietly said to herself as she removed the tiny, frayed black notebook from the bottom of a shoebox from Wagner Shoes. Opening it she immediately recognized her mom's handwriting, although here on the pages it looked nothing like the elegant script she was used to seeing. Here it looked like it had been written in a rushed manner.

1964

Sam is not who he says he is. I just know it. There's something he's hiding, something he's not telling me. How could he do this to me, to our family?

Is he even Jewish? Is his real name even Sam?

Who really is this man I married?

1965

I don't understand why Sam was so upset with the Frankfurt Auschwitz trials. I asked him one evening, "Isn't it good these camp guards are finally being brought to justice, being held accountable for their actions all those years before? For all the lives they took, the lives they destroyed." And all he could say to me was "Let the past stay in the past, what's done is done." Saying this like he was talking about a matter of no importance, and not the deaths of six million of our people including his very own parents and sister. And then he said what was chilling most of all. "What, they think because they got Eichmann in '60 they're going to get us all?" I stood at him dumbfounded. "What?" he said to me. "You said us," I told him. "Not them." "Of course I said them," he angrily replied, "why would I have said us? Now you're accusing me of saying something I never did," and he stormed out of the bedroom, slamming the door behind him.

But I know what I heard. He said __us.__

1966
He has the tattoo, of course he's Jewish.

1966
Maybe he's not Jewish, was he just a regular prisoner of the Nazis? I know they imprisoned so many non-Jews, was he a political prisoner? Is he really Catholic? I hope he wasn't a homosexual, oy vey.

1971
Twenty years of marriage and we only have one photograph of the two of us. It's like he doesn't want his picture taken…ever. As if he's permanently in hiding from something.

Becky closed the little black book and then her eyes, struggling to grasp what she had just read. But then curious if there were more entries like that, she flipped through the rest of the pages but they were all blank. The last entry had been the one made in 1971, nearly 30 years ago.

Taking this as reassurance that her mom had been wrong about her dad, her heart returned to a normal pace until she wondered to herself, "But then why had she never gotten rid of this little book? Why had she kept it all this time in a place she had clearly never wanted my dad to find out about?" And then the one obvious fact-the pages were worn and lightly frayed, almost as if a person had constantly been flipping through its pages, back and forth.

❧ CHAPTER 11 ❧

Berlin, Germany
2006

"Entschuldigung, wann ist der nächste zug?"

Becky looked up to see a woman around her age with olive colored skin and dark curly hair standing before her. She had been so engrossed in attempting to translate the words on the pages of the children's book *Aschenputtel* (Cinderella) she had picked up earlier that morning that she hadn't even seen the woman approach her. Probably not the wisest thing to be doing in the relatively deserted Mendelssohn-Bartholdy-Park U-Bahn station, she thought to herself, as the woman still stared at her expectantly, waiting for a response.

"Oh, I'm sorry, I don't speak German," Becky said.

"You're not German?" the woman asked in slightly surprised, accented English.

"No, American," Becky answered, feeling pathetic over her monolingual abilities.

"I just thought with your looks," the woman said, her words trailing off.

"My looks, what?" Becky asked, unsure where the woman had been going with her comment.

"You just look like you could have been on one of those propaganda posters from the '30s, you know the ones of the blond hair, blue eyed women, wearing the traditional *dirndl,* bestowing flowers and kisses to the brave and valiant Wehrmacht solider."

Was the woman trying to be funny, Becky wondered? If so, she had a messed up sense of humor.

"I'm German. Well, my father is. He immigrated to the US after the war."

"Ahh, of course he did," the woman replied sardonically.

"What's that supposed to mean?" Becky asked defensively, incredulous that she was getting drawn into some messed up weird conversation with a stranger in a Berlin U-Bahn station.

"Well, my parents were German too, they immigrated to Israel after the war. But mine got to Israel by way of surviving four years of hell in the camps. Let me guess, your dad was actually a Wehrmacht soldier after all? A German soldier who just got out scot-free?"

Hurriedly standing up, Becky said angrily, "No, you stereotyping asshole. He was actually in Auschwitz for three years. The tattoo on his arm and the loss of his parents and his sister to the Nazis was not exactly a scot-free war-time experience."

She headed towards the exit but not before turning around and saying over her shoulder, *"Fahr zur Hölle."*

Becky had never before told off anyone in her life but it sure felt good just then to tell that woman to go to hell.

Over her meal that night of milk-fed rotisserie chicken and tangy German-style potato and white cabbage salads at Henne, a historic restaurant on the Moritzplatz someone in Pittsburgh had recommended she try, Becky reflected on her first full day in the city of her father's birth.

In Munich, a city she had no connection to, she had allowed herself to play the role of tourist, which she had genuinely enjoyed. Here in Berlin, it was different. She wasn't a tourist but rather a visitor. She had come to the German capital to learn about her past, the past of her father but also to unearth the ghosts of her aunt and grandparents.

Although on the night she had arrived in Berlin, she had rushed off to visit the Memorial to the Murdered Jews of Europe, Becky had become emotionally overwhelmed when she realized that the names of her grandparents and aunt could be three of the three million names of Holocaust victims inscribed in the Place of Information below the Memorial. She decided then that she would take her first full day in Berlin to have nothing to do with the war, the Holocaust, or her own family's ties and past to the city.

She had begun her day with a walk through the Tiergarten, the city's famous urban green oasis. What had started off as a pleasant outing turned into one of sadness when staring at the park benches, she imagined the words *"Juden Ist Die Benutzung der Parkbank Verboten,"* painted on them. She had seen so many pictures of life in Nazi Germany when the rights of Jewish citizens were stripped further and further, including something as simple and taken for granted as the act of sitting on a park bench.

She was more than happy to leave the park behind when she spotted the majestic Quadriga, the famous statue of the goddess of victory driving a chariot pulled by four horses that rested atop the Brandenburg Gate, through the top of the tree line.

It was standing at this momentous symbol, one of peace and unity today, but tumult and discord in times past, that Becky felt tears forming. Unlike at Dachau when she had cried in the room that housed all of the stolen possessions of the prisoners that had passed through the camp's gate, here they were tears of happiness that she was finally present, in a place she had dreamt about visiting for so long. Naturally these same happy tears were promptly forgotten about less than an hour later following the upsetting encounter with the arrogant stranger in the U-Bahn station.

Even after heading over to East Berlin, where she first sampled the city's most famous street food, currywurst, trying it both *mit darm* (with casing) and *ohne darm* (without casing) per the recommendation of the pleasant and charming vendor, and then walking the length of the Eastside Gallery, the series of murals that were painted directly onto a long remnant of the Berlin Wall, Becky still couldn't shake the hurtfulness of the woman's presumption about her, about her father, and all because of her looks.

But then that night at dinner, as she waited for her check, she removed from her tote bag the small, weathered black notebook that had been one of the first things she had packed for her trip. She flipped to the page with the 1965 entry, the one that had the words on it-

> *"What, they think because they got Eichmann in '60 they're going to get us all?" I stood at him dumbfounded. "What?" he said to me. "You said us," I told him. "Not them." "Of course I said them," he angrily replied, "why would I have said us? Now you're accusing me of saying something I never did," and he stormed out of the bedroom, slamming the door behind him. But I know what I heard. He said **us.***

⚜ CHAPTER 12 ⚜

Berlin, Germany
2006

Considering that her own father's childhood had been one of privilege and wealth, Becky had no ties to Scheunenviertel, the former Jewish quarter of the city that up until the Second World War had been considered a slum. It was during the 20th century that the area grew enormously, thanks to the mass immigration of Hasidic Jews from Eastern Europe, many of whom had trouble assimilating with the more liberal existing Jewish community, the community that her own family had once belonged to.

Becky had read that starting in the late 1600s, the district had become the heart of the city's Jewish community and so she couldn't help but think that perhaps at one time, hundreds of years ago even, some of her ancestors had once lived here and walked these same streets. And this seemed like a good enough reason as any to come here. Of course today most traces of Jewish life and culture were long gone, replaced by hip boutiques and eateries and a gentrified clientele from the looks of it.

But her real reason for taking the S-Bahn that morning to the Hackescher Markt station was to visit the nearby *Neue Synagoge,* the synagogue she had first heard about on her 13th birthday, the first time ever in her life that her father had spoken to Becky about his childhood.

As she stood standing on *Oranienburger Straße* across the street from the synagogue, gazing up at its elaborate gilded dome that looked more like it belonged in Arabia than the streets of Berlin (a nod to Alhambra Palace, which it was modeled after), Becky's eyes settled on the space by the front doors. She closed her eyes for a moment and tried to picture her grandparents, aunt, and father walking down the street, ready to go in for services on the High Holy Days as the type of getaway vehicles the likes of Bonnie Parker and Clyde Barrow would have driven following their bank heists drove by. Her grandfather cut a dashing figure in a suit and matching fedora (which he would exchange for a *yarmulke* upon entering, of course) while her grandmother, beautiful and elegant as any 1930s movie star, was dressed in a peach-colored dress with matching white kid gloves and hat that she wore at a side angle. And then there was her Aunt Marta, a mirror image of her mother in both dress and looks followed by Becky's father, a blond haired schoolboy who wasn't quite old enough for long pants yet.

Becky opened her eyes once more, back now in the 21st century after her brief visit to 1930s Berlin. She crossed the street now to stand directly in front of what had once been the main place of worship for the city's thriving Jewish population, the largest synagogue in all of Germany. She still couldn't believe that a building as majestic and grandiose as this, one that exemplified Jewish life in the German capital, had survived the terrible events of *Kristallnacht* only to be destroyed by Allied bombing five years later in 1943.

A small plaque on the front of the building appeared to be a memorial marker about the synagogue during the war. It was entirely in German but she could understand a few words here and there. But there was one phrase she absolutely knew the meaning of, "*Vergesst es nie.*" Becky had spent enough years reading about the Holocaust to know the German for "never forget."

"You are Jewish."

Becky had just left the synagogue and was still standing on *Oranienburger Straße* studying her map of the city when she heard the faint voice from behind her, coming from the synagogue. She turned around to see a petite elderly woman with a blond (presumably dyed) bob, perhaps around her father's age, smiling at her. Becky started to respond that yes she was but then stopped herself, realizing the woman hadn't asked it but rather stated it. Like she already knew.

"Wait, how did you know I'm Jewish?" Becky asked incredulously. "Since I got here everyone assumed I was German."

"What, because Jews can only have thick dark hair, big noses, and bushy eyebrows?" the woman replied, half-raising her eyebrow at Becky.

"No, that's not at all what I-"

The old woman interrupted Becky then, placing her weathered and gnarled hand atop hers and said, "*Liebling*, I know you meant nothing by it. But inside, I heard you saying the *El Malei Rachamim*."

The prayer for the soul of the deceased. The prayer she had uttered just moments before, praying for the souls of her grandparents and aunt.

"Are you off to anywhere?"

Unsure if she should lie about her plans to the woman since she was after all a complete stranger, Becky realized she was being silly since the elderly woman looked like she barely weighed 100 pounds and was a couple of inches shorter than Becky's five foot five frame.

"I was planning to find a café, maybe get a coffee and a piece of *apfelstrudel,*" Becky said honestly, unsure what she planned to do or go to next. She figured a slice of warm and delicious apple strudel was the best form of motivational planning.

"There's someplace I'd like to show you," the woman said to Becky. "It's not too far from here." She started to walk away then, only to turn around and say to Becky, "come."

Okay, maybe the old woman wasn't physically menacing but neither was the witch (at first) in Hansel and Gretel…she was in Germany after all.

Still waiting for Becky a few feet ahead, looking like she was going to place her hands on her hips any moment in an exasperated fashion, Becky hurried up to meet the woman. And off they went to parts (hopefully safe) unknown…

"You would never know it but this was once Berlin's oldest Jewish cemetery," the old woman said to Becky, her eyes vacant, her voice emotionless as she stared ahead at the small fenced park.

"But where are all the graves? I don't see any markers," Becky asked, not quite understanding what she was looking at.

"A few of the old gravestones can still be seen in the cemetery wall," the old woman said, still looking straight ahead. "But in 1943, the SS completely destroyed it, by orders of the Gestapo. 12,000 members of the city's first Jewish community were buried here for almost 200 years only for the tombstones to be smashed to pieces by the SS thugs."

She paused then, two identical tears silently running down her cheek.

"Berlin's first home for the elderly was here, but during the war it served as a deportation camp. I'll never forget seeing them playing football with the skulls."

Becky said nothing, feelings of horror and disbelief rising within her.

"Most tourists to Berlin, they want to see the Wall, drink big strong beers, do a Hitler themed bunker tour. But they don't see this," she said, waving her hands at what was once a cemetery. "They don't want to be depressed by the past, especially something like the Holocaust. But I could tell you were different. Because you have a tie to it, I could tell."

"My father was a survivor. Of the camps," she added like it was some extra badge of horrific courage.

"The rest of your family?" the woman asked.

"He was the only one." Becky didn't have to say the words "who survived." It was understood.

"Come *libeling*," the old woman said. "I will tell you my story now, over a delicious slice of *apfelstrudel* at a place that very few tourists know about."

⚜

It was over a slice of *apfelstrudel* and a plate of *zwetschgenknoedel* they shared that Ursula had insisted upon, saying it was the best plum dumplings Becky would ever have (by now they had finally properly introduced themselves to one another) when she told Becky her own wartime story.

"I had blond hair just like yours when I was younger," Ursula said to Becky. "Well, that is naturally speaking," she said, her eyes twinkling. "What you see now," waving her hand over her elegantly coiffed head, "is all thanks to a certain Monsieur L'Oréal."

Turning serious she added, "My hair is what kept me alive during the war. It's what allowed me to pass as a non-Jew after I went underground."

"Underground?" Becky asked, a term she was not familiar with.

Gone into hiding, sure, but underground?

"Yes, we Jews who were not permanently hidden during the war. We actually called ourselves U-boats, because we were constantly having to come 'above the surface' for things like food, money, and most often, new places to stay." Continuing on she said, "There were more good Germans than you'd think." Seeing Becky's quizzical expression she added, "you know, those who didn't agree with the Nazis, who didn't like what was happening to the Jews. So those types of people, they hid Jews, but often for just a few nights, never long-term. They were too afraid of the risks of being discovered, of being ratted out, basically of having what was happening to the Jews happen to them and their families. So that was the absolute worst of being a U-boat, constantly looking for a new place to sleep at night, constantly having to depend, no, put your trust in someone else to help you."

"And you were a U-boat for the entire war?" Becky asked incredulously.

"As I said, my blond hair helped. My sister though, she was not so lucky." Ursula stopped talking then, pained, it seemed, from remembering the past.

"It's okay, you don't need to keep talking about it," Becky said, hoping she sounded reassuring to this sweet old lady who had been through so much.

"Thank you my dear," Ursula said, smiling at her as she lightly patted her hand "but I know I am strong enough to continue."

"Well, take your time," Becky told her. "Because meeting you might truly be the highlight of my entire trip." And she meant it. She had yet to truly delve into her father's own personal story here in Berlin but meeting a woman like Ursula who, unlike her father DID want to share her past with others, with a complete stranger no less, meant so much to Becky. It was a random, chance encounter, one she'd never forget.

"By the time Hitler came to power in '33 my parents were already dead. My mother had died of cancer when I was a child and my father was killed in a tram accident in '31. So it was just my sister and me. Me taking after our mother with my blond hair and blue eyes and my younger sister taking after our father, with his thick dark curly hair and brown eyes. You see my father wasn't German. Well, that is to say, he hadn't been born here in Germany. He came here from Poland when he was a small child; they settled in Scheunenviertel. Germany was the only place he truly ever knew, ever was home to him. His family disowned him when he married my mother, a non-Jew, as German as they come. They were poor, we were poor, but we were always happy."

"When the Nazis came to power, strangers didn't believe Kadi and I were sisters since we looked nothing alike. And in time I know she started resenting me, hating that people considered me German whereas she was perhaps a lowly immigrant from Eastern Europe."

"Did she try to pass too? Was she also a U-boat?" Becky asked, curious about what had happened to Kadi.

"One day I came home to our apartment in Scheunenviertel, where we had lived with our parents, and she was just gone. As if she had never existed." Wiping a tear from her cheek she almost whispered, "She had received her deportation order and never told me. She went to her death and never told her own sister."

"I'm so sorry, Ursula," Becky said, wanting to comfort the now upset and crying older woman.

"I've told this story hundreds of times now but it never gets easier. Never once."

"And that's when you went underground then?" Becky asked.

"Yes, Kadi was part of the first group of Berlin Jews to be deported. She boarded a train at *Bahnhof* Grunewald on October 18, 1941 for Lizmannstadt, or Lodz as I think most of the world knows it, and I, Ursula Frydman, ceased to exist. My sister was dying of hunger and sickness in the ghetto and I was passing as an Aryan woman. I was Jutta Müller."

Becky wanted to say 'you did what you had to do to survive' but what right did she have to say words so callous and empty as these? She may be the daughter of a Holocaust survivor but survivor's guilt was an emotion she could never in a million years fully understand.

"And you know something? They even made the Jews they were deporting pay for their fare. They were being sent to their deaths but they still charged everyone over the age of 10 per kilometer four *pfennigs* or pennies I think you call them. The fare to die."

Becky was speechless. She didn't think anything could have been more upsetting than hearing how the SS played football with the skulls from graves and yet requiring Jews who were being deported to pay for their train fare or deeper into the war, their journey on freight wagons.

"My father…he…," Becky stammered, "he never really talked about the war, about what he went through. I never understood this, why he wouldn't want his own daughter to know about it."

Now being the one to play the role of comforter, Ursula took Becky's hand in hers and said, "It was his way of dealing with it, *libeling*. There are the survivors like me, who share, who go to school visits, who meet with newspapermen to make sure what happened is never forgotten and then there are the survivors like your father who were able to start again simply by choosing to keep what had happened in the past and by not talking about it. No one is braver than the other."

Seeing her father in an entirely new light now, Becky thought to herself, truer words had never been spoken.

Becky sadly parted with Ursula following their unhealthy lunch of pastries and coffee at the wonderfully untouristy and very authentic café in Scheunenviertel. Ursula had told her "I don't do the email but," handing Becky a small piece of paper she said, "here is my address and phone number. Please keep in touch, *libeling*. Oh, and you must visit the *Topographie des Terrors*, the Topography of Terror."

"The what?" Becky asked, not knowing at all what the older woman was referring to.

"It's a most fascinating museum. It focuses on the perpetrators rather than the victims. In Mitte," the central Berlin neighborhood where Becky was staying.

And then as if she were Baroness Schraeder from the 1965 film *The Sound of Music* kissing Captain Von Trapp goodbye so he could be with his true love Maria, Ursula leaned forward, kissed Becky on the cheek while saying the words, *auf wiedersehen,* and walked away.

But all Becky could think about was that she had no desire whatsoever to visit a museum whose sole focus was on the Nazis and the SS. How could Ursula have even suggested such a thing?

But that night after a filling meal of *eisbein,* boiled ham hock with sauerkraut and mashed potatoes with bacon, a typical Berlin dish the waiter had told her, she decided to visit the *Topographie des Terrors*. Especially after the desk clerk at her hotel told her that it was a most impressive history museum, one very much worth checking out. The fact that there was no admission cost also swayed her in visiting the museum that was located on the site of the buildings which, among other organizations, had housed the Gestapo headquarters.

As Becky walked along the relatively deserted *Niederkirchnerstraße* to the museum, she couldn't help but feel a little creeped out. To think she was walking on the same street that cars had transported people who had been arrested to Gestapo Headquarters where they would be tortured and/or killed, the majority never walking out alive again onto *Niederkirchnerstraße*.

When it started to rain lightly, Becky pulled the hood of her jacket up over her already disheveled hair and muttered, "Are you kidding me?" Although in truth the light, misting rain only made the deserted street that had borne witness to so much evil and horror seem that much more sinister.

Ursula had been right. The museum was fascinating. Becky had tried reading every word found within the three main permanent exhibits but started skimming and looking more at the pictures and accompanying captions when an announcement sounded reminding visitors that the museum would be closing soon.

It was by chance that Becky saw the black and white photograph. She had been hurrying along, anxious to make sure she had time to check out the special exhibit on The Trial of Major War Criminals in Nuremberg (an ode to her father and his penchant for always wanting her to be the next Cecilia Goetz) when she saw it. A photo with a caption that read "Laughing at Auschwitz-SS auxiliaries pose at a resort for Auschwitz personnel, 1945" and a man standing on the far left who looked exactly like…her father.

❧ CHAPTER 13 ❧

Berlin, Germany
2006

"Talk about a doppelgänger," Becky thought to herself as she leaned in for a closer look at this haunting photograph. People having a great time without a care in the world while innocent men, women, and children were being gassed, starved, and beaten. She continued staring at the photo, wondering what it was about the man in the photo that seemed so familiar to her. She gasped when it came to her.

It wasn't just the style of the man's blond hair or his big ears or even his face. It was the way he was standing. The same way her father stood in his wedding portrait with her mom, the only photograph that existed of him. Awkwardly posing, his left arm hanging straight at his side, not embracing the girls he was standing next to, almost as if he was shy, while his right arm was slightly bent, as if he was holding it open for someone to sneak in right before the flash went off.

Growing up, she often would sneak looks at her parents' wedding portrait when her father wasn't home, when she knew it was safe to go into their bedroom, for he never allowed it to be on display where company could potentially see it. The one (and only) time she'd asked why this was, he'd snapped at her and said, "Mind your own damn business," to which *bubbe* had scolded him for swearing. But she had always found it odd that her father would pose so awkwardly in his wedding portrait. It wasn't that he looked stiff; it was more like he seemed unsure of himself, like he didn't really belong there. Like this man in this picture seemed to be.

Her mom's handwritten words came to her again-

"What, they think because they got Eichmann in '60 they're going to get us all?"

My god, Becky thought as she stumbled over to a nearby bench, immediately slumping down onto it, not caring a fig if people thought she was drunk which is most likely how she looked to anyone in the museum who saw her. All those years her mom had always suspected something didn't quite add up about Samuel Weiss' supposed past, that there was something he never told his wife and daughter, that it was simply too dark and big a secret to EVER tell anyone. Judy's entries in her notebook had stopped because she had never been able to find that missing piece of the puzzle. But Becky had found it and now it was staring her straight in the face.

And before she could be sick, she ran off in search of a bathroom, not able to look another second at the awkward looking man posing on the far left of the photograph.

The next two days Becky walked around in a daze. She ate little, subsisting mostly on black coffee and rolls that she had hoarded from the hotel's continental breakfast spread. Things she had planned to see and do-visit the Jewish Museum, take a day trip to Potsdam-she did none of them because all she could think about, the only thing she could focus on, was the photograph she had seen and what it meant.

Her father hadn't just taken on a new identity because of the war. He had become someone else because he'd had to hide who he was, and had been, a war criminal. Her mom, who had been one of the proudest Jews you would have ever met, had been married for almost half a century to a Nazi. And Judy had been right, ever since she wrote that first entry in the little worn black notebook, she had been right that Becky's father had been hiding something, that he had not been who he said he was. Her mom had always suspected, she just didn't have the proof that Becky got from seeing that chilling photo. Her father had never allowed his picture to be taken out of fear that someone would recognize him, would tie him to Auschwitz. Even after he had an ocean separating him from Europe as well as the passage of time, his deep-rooted fear and paranoia always remained. That one day, somehow, he'd be caught.

She knew he wasn't really Samuel Weiss. So who was he?

On her final day in Berlin, Becky roused herself enough to do two things. First, she went back to the *Topographie des Terrors* and photographed it…the picture of her father. She didn't know how or when or even if she would confront him but she needed to have this photo, this piece of evidence. And then she went to *Kroenstraße,* the street where her father had lived as a child and young man…or said he did.

Before seeing the picture, she had put off visiting *Kroenstraße* for fear it would be too emotional, too much of a tangible tie to her dead grandparents and aunt she had never known, never had the chance to know. But now, it was different. Because was anything she had been told by her father actually true? Or was the apartment on *Kroenstraße* just another one of his lies?

One of the things Becky loved most about Berlin was that, at least in Mitte, there were placards everywhere that told you about what had once "stood there." She knew enough from reading that the city had been heavily damaged from Allied bombings and then of course during the Battle of Berlin in the waning days of the war. So she appreciated these placards that allowed her to close her eyes and picture what had once stood there. She only wished there had been one such placard for *Kroenstraße* for when Becky got there, all she saw were generic, post-war buildings. Nothing like the Art Nouveau building she had once imagined.

As she started to walk away, heading back in the direction of *Gendarmenmarkt*, the famous historical market square where she planned to enjoy her final beer on German soil (she was leaning towards a *dunkel*, a dark German lager she had grown an affinity for since being here), she happened to look down and saw four gold colored square stones that looked to be permanently affixed to the pavement. When she knelt down to look more closely, she saw they contained text, but nearly lost balance when she noticed the names-Benjamin Weiss, Giselle Weiss, Marta Weiss, and...Samuel Weiss?

She recognized the names of places like Dachau and Ghetto Lizmannstadt (wait, hadn't Ursula told her that was the German name for Lodz?) and the German word for deported (*deportiert*) then wondered about the meaning of the words *"hier wohnte"* since all four of the squares had them. She froze upon reading the square for Samuel Weiss-

Ermordet in Auschwitz

"*Ermordet…ermordet…*"Becky whispered over and over to herself. "What does that mean?"

"Excuse me, but can you tell me what the word *ermordet* means?" Becky said to her waiter as he placed the huge stein of beer she had ordered down onto the table where she was seated.

"Hmm, you're into a bit of a dark topic," he said jokingly.

"Why?" Becky asked, not understanding the humor.

"It means murdered."

"Oh," Becky replied, the first sip of beer she had just taken now starting to come back up her throat in the form of bile. "I, um," she began, taking her camera out of her purse and turning it on. "I found these today, *ermordet* was a word on it," handing her camera to the affable waiter who seemed eager to talk to her in the otherwise deserted café.

"Oh, these are *stolpersteine*. I see now why you wanted to know about *ermordet*. Don't worry, I no longer think you are weird," he said with a smile.

"*Stolper* what?" Becky asked, not able to pronounce the word the waiter had just rattled off.

"In German they mean 'stumbling stone' or some people call them 'stumbling blocks' meaning you literally stumble over them like you probably did." At Becky's blank look he continued, "They are a form of Holocaust memorial, to the Jews. A German artist dude, he started this project back in the '90s. He placed these blocks where Jews used to live, and they say the person's name, when they were born, when they were deported, and if known, when they died.

"There are more of these in Berlin?" Becky asked.

"Oh yes, but not just Berlin, and not just Germany. I think there are now ones in the Netherlands and Austria too."

"But people don't see them. I mean, they can so easily miss them, overlook them."

"But you didn't," the waiter said. "I think having them like they are, it's more, how do you say in English…um…jarring, yes, when you do see them. When you are confronted with, this is where a victim lived. Right here where you are standing. A collective memorial is great, but what does that say about the individual?"

"*Helmut!* An angry yell emanated from the kitchen, followed by an even angrier and impatient sounding, "*Ich brauche deine hilfe!*"

"Sorry miss, I have to get back to work," the kind waiter told her.

"No, I'm so sorry," Becky answered, feeling bad for having gotten him in trouble. "I didn't mean to keep you."

"No problem," he said and with that he was gone, headed towards the kitchen to undoubtedly await a tongue lashing.

"*Ermordet in Auschwitz,*" Becky whispered to herself again. Murdered in Auschwitz. And yet, the man she knew as Samuel Weiss was alive and well in Pittsburgh, Pennsylvania.

CHAPTER 14

Pittsburgh, Pennsylvania
2006

"Elderly man is arrested for Nazi war crimes after daughter turns him in"

"Man claiming to be Holocaust survivor is in fact a former concentration camp guard"

"Daughter atones for father's wartime crimes by turning him in to the authorities "

These were just some of the headlines that Becky envisioned being splashed across the front pages of newspapers and Internet news sites if she were to come forward and turn her father into the authorities. Although at this point she wasn't even sure who she'd turn him in to-the FBI? Interpol? The German government? She had no clue because frankly, she had been emotionally drowning in these thoughts for weeks now.

The first week or so that she was back and had returned to work, Becky was able to chalk up her forgetting things, her spacing out, her not being able to concentrate, on jet lag. But now, after having been back for almost three weeks, she knew that wouldn't really be plausible any longer.

Since she had been back in Pittsburgh, she had resumed her weekly visits to her father's house and still called to check in on him twice a week too. But she didn't do anything beyond that. She stopped trying to initiate conversations with him when she was at his house. And the twice weekly telephone conversations consisted of her asking if he needed anything and, if he had happened to go to the doctor's that week, to ask him how the visit went and what the doctor had said. But she allowed for nothing more to be said, always being the one to steer the conversation in the tone and direction she wanted and of course, ending it when she wanted. If he noticed the cold change within her, he said nothing. But then confronting a person was clearly not something he was comfortable doing.

"Hey, Becky!"

Becky turned around upon hearing her name called out, wondering where it was coming from, when she noticed a man walking towards her on Liberty Avenue. She couldn't think where she knew the man from until she realized it was Adam from her survivors' group meetings.

"Oh, hi Adam," Becky said, feeling a bit awkward, especially considering the circumstances in which they had met.

"Doing some shopping?" he asked, arching his eyebrow at her hands which were laden with groceries from Donatelli's and Groceria Italiana.

"Yep, the only Jew you'll ever meet who likes Italian food as much as any Italian," she said laughingly.

He laughed in kind but then, studying her face, asked, "Do you live around here?"

"Um, yeah, my apartment's just two blocks away," she answered, hoping she sounded vague and indifferent.

"Any interest in grabbing a cup a coffee? Talking perhaps about some lighter topics?" a playful jab of course to the very serious and sometimes upsetting and disturbing talks they had in their monthly Second Generation meetings.

"Um, well, I really need to get these groceries home and put away," she said, hoping he'd take the hint.

"Well, I can help you with that. That's why I asked if you lived close by."

The man had an answer for everything, it seemed. She knew she would need to come up with a plausible excuse in the next few seconds as to why she couldn't do a coffee date with him when she stopped herself. The man had been nothing but kind to her ever since her first meeting at the Second Generation group. But it was just being around someone like him, someone who truly was the child of an actual Holocaust survivor, that wracked her with guilt, and a situation she wanted to avoid putting herself in. But right now, she couldn't say no to him.

"Sure, that would be great. I'm just up this way," indicating with her head to Cedar Street.

"Gosh, I'm sorry," he said reaching out to take her bags. "Where are my manners?"

And with that one act of simple yet sadly outdated chivalry, Becky became unwillingly smitten with Adam Lefkovitz.

⚜

"I hope you won't mind me asking this but is something the matter?"

She had been on five dates with Adam by then, not counting their first unofficial afternoon coffee date where they had ended up talking for nearly two hours. The problem was she liked him...a lot in fact.

She just didn't know how he felt about her in that way, outside of a "we met in a children of Holocaust survivors' support group," which is not exactly the clique anyone wants to really be in and certainly doesn't scream out things like romance and love of one's life.

"Umm, no," Becky answered quickly, starting to feel a pang of anxiety take over her that somehow she had messed this up, the closest thing to a relationship she had had since her divorce. Paining her to ask she said, "Have I done something wrong?"

"Oh no, gosh no Becky, I didn't mean it like that," he told her reassuringly, covering her now probably slightly clammy hand with his. "I just meant you seem like there's always something on your mind, always something troubling you. You just so often look like you're thousands of miles away with your thoughts. If you say you're good, that there's nothing wrong, then I believe you, matter is dropped," he told her, lacing her fingers with his and squeezing her hand then.

"Can we go back to my apartment after dinner? Skip the movie, I mean?" she asked, knowing that if she were to ever have a relationship with Adam, if it were to ever grow and develop into something more, then she would have to tell him the truth, the horrible, sinister secret she had discovered in Germany.

"How do you know I'm that kind of man?" he asked jokingly.

When she didn't laugh and he noticed her pained expression, he said, "Of course. Whatever you want to do."

"It's just that…"she trailed off. "There's something I need to tell you."

"You're saying you think your dad was a Nazi, worked at Auschwitz, simply from the way he's standing in two pictures?" Adam asked incredulously, holding the copies of both her parents' wedding photo and the one she had taken from the *Topographie des Terrors* side-by-side in his hands. "I mean, that's a bit of a stretch, wouldn't you say?"

"Never mind the absolute identical appearance. But when you pair that with this bizarre way of posing? I know that's my father," Becky said.

"You said he has a tattoo. You're telling me some Nazi camp guard willingly did that to himself?"

"If it meant evading capture from the Allies at the end of the war? To avoid being tried as a war criminal and put in jail? Yes. I can believe that of my father and anyone else not wanting to be caught."

"Does your father have the SS blood type tattoo?"

"A what?" Becky asked, unsure of what he was referring to.

"SS soldiers often had their blood type tattooed on the underside of their arm, usually near the armpit. That way if they were ever wounded, doctors would immediately know their blood type. And post-war it was a way for the Allies to flush out SS who were trying to pose as innocent civilians or in some cases, Jews, after making their way to displaced persons camps."

"I don't know, I never saw anything like that," she answered truthfully.

"Well, it might not matter much anyway. I read a while ago that towards the end of the war, when it was clear Germany was losing, they stopped doing it. So if your father was in the SS, he might not have ever had it at all depending on when he enlisted."

"There's also this," Becky said, handing him the small, decades old, worn black notebook. "There's not much to read, but please read it. I think afterwards you'll clearly see why I think it's him."

Starting to walk towards the kitchen she asked over her shoulder, "Can I fix you a nightcap?"

"Sure, he said, his eyes not looking up from the page he was reading.

"Manhattan?" she asked.

"Sure," his attention now entirely focused on the words before him.

"What do I do?" Becky whispered to him, nestled in his arms. They were lying on her bed by then, still fully clothed, and still wide awake after having talked for hours since returning from dinner.

When she had handed him the Manhattan she had prepared, he had taken it from her, downed it, and said thanks. Then he had led her to her bedroom where he just held her and continued to do so.

"I honestly have no idea, Becky. I mean, God, when I asked you earlier if something was bothering you, I never in a million years would have imagined this."

He said the last word like it carried some contagious disease. That from merely saying it out loud, it would infect his thoughts like it had Becky's.

"I'm so sorry to have involved you in this," she said, her voice emotionally fraught. "Especially considering how we met and God, your mom's own personal experiences during the war. I just-" she broke off then, unable to continue.

"Hey," he said, turning her around so that she was facing him, looking up at his handsome profile. "None of that, you hear me? I know we've only gone on a few dates but..." taking a deep breath he continued, "I'm really starting to have feelings for you, Becky. So, there's nothing I wouldn't do for you, and nothing I would shy away from if it concerns you."

He lightly grazed her cheeks with the tips of his fingers. "And I mean this. What our parents went through during the war, their experiences, their stories, they have nothing to do with us. For too long I let the Holocaust define who I was. Well, I'm not about to let it define my personal relationship with you. If your father was indeed a Nazi, you don't have any part in that, you had nothing to do with it. No child should ever have to pay for the sins of the parent."

And with that Becky was a puddle of emotional, sentimental mud. Whereas her relationship and subsequent marriage to Danny had been one of rebellion, the urge to go against the wishes of her father, to assert herself in the face of his controlling and dominating nature, twenty years later she was not the same person she had been then. She was undoubtedly more mature but also she was finally and truly her own person. Defined by no one except herself.

✤ CHAPTER 15 ✤

Pittsburgh, Pennsylvania
2006

Adam's ultimate advice had been to read up on the prosecution of former Nazis who had been caught and tried long after the war had ended. "And no," he had told her, "I don't mean those at the level of Eichman or Stangl," the latter referring to "the White Death," the former commander of the Treblinka death camp in Poland. "I'm talking about your average Joe SS soldiers, camp guards, and see if the world cared enough after the war ended, after even the Germanys were reunified, to dredge up the painful past through prosecution."

So that's what she did, even enlisting the help of Cece, a childhood friend of hers who had become a librarian and now worked the reference desk at the main branch of the Carnegie Library.

After her doing her thing on the computer accessing the apparently digital catalog (Becky did not say to Cece that the last time she had been in a library the old card catalog was still in existence), her friend had recommended she check out titles like Simon Wiesenthal's *Justice not Vengeance* and *I Chased Eichmann: A True Story* and Deborah Lipstadt's *Denying the Holocaust*.

"I have no interest in the Holocaust, I mean it's too sad and all, there's enough sadness in the world, but even I had to read it after the famous trial," Cece had said.

"Trial?" Becky asked, unsure of what she was referring to.

"Don't you read the papers?" her friend retorted. "I thought you were as much a book nerd as I was in school. Anyhow, this woman, Lipstadt, wrote this book about the Holocaust denial movement. Well, one of the people in it that she named as a denier, he ended up suing her for libel! Can you imagine? Your feelings are well-known and documented just about everywhere, but you sue someone because you feel you've been defamed. Well, he lost, thank goodness. What an asshole."

"Thanks, Cece," Becky said, ready to take her leave.

"Did you go back to school or something?" Cece asked casually, her eyes already back on her computer screen as she typed away absentmindedly.

Becky paused, for a second realizing that Cece clearly didn't remember that Becky was Jewish, let alone had a father who had survived the Holocaust. "Umm, yeah, in a way," Becky answered, hoping she sounded casual enough. "I'm taking a course at CCAC, just for fun, no credits or anything."

"Oh, cool," Cece replied, her eyes still glued to her monitor screen. "Well, good seeing you again Becky, keep in touch."

"Sure, and thanks again," Becky said, saying the words so softly she doubted her friend had even heard.

Pittsburgh, Pennsylvania
1969

"Do you think Dad can come to my school and talk about the Holocaust?" Becky asked her mom as they both sat in the kitchen,

Becky working on her French homework while her mom was preparing dinner.

There was a still moment before Judy answered, "I don't think that's such a good idea, honey."

"Yeah, but right now in Mr. Gormon's class we're covering World War II, well, actually right now we just got to the Third Reich, so we're in the 1930s, you know the years building up to the war. And wouldn't it be awesome if someone who had lived through all of that, I mean, and survived Hitler, the Nazis, the camps, could come to my class and talk about it? I mean, the kids would think I was the coolest ever." Becky said this last part in a way that only a clueless, slightly self-absorbed teenager could do.

"Your father is a very private man, especially about his experiences during the war," her mom said to Becky, her back still to her as she stood at the stove stirring a pot of spaghetti sauce.

"Yeah, but maybe the reason that he's this way is that he keeps it all bottled up inside him," Becky retorted, not wanting to take no for an answer, and secretly desperate to do something, anything really, that would make the cool kids notice her. So far her freshman year at Taylor Allderdice had been filled with nothing but a whole lot of teen angst, compounded by the fact that she wasn't allowed to have much of a social life; well, no social life.

"Becky honey, please. The dead are resting," Judy said wearily.

"What is that even supposed to mean?" Becky grumbled under her breath, as she stared for what seemed to be the umpteenth time at the *passé compose*, still not understanding a lick of why or when you were supposed to use this stupid tense.

"So Dad, do you think in the coming weeks you could come to my school and speak to my history class? About your experiences during the war?" Becky asked brightly, not caring at all that she had just blatantly gone against her mom's wishes.

Both her mom and dad's forks clattered loudly to their plates at the same time and then the air grew so quiet you could have heard a pin drop. Judy looked at her aghast, almost with a pained expression that could be translated to, "Why did you go there?" while her dad's expression breathed anger and fury, his eyes a dark and menacing shade of blue, his skin having turned a bright, reddened hue.

Ever since her 13th birthday the year before, when he had broken down in front of her as they sat together inside Rodef Shalom while he recounted memories of his dead parents and sister, he hadn't said a single thing to her about his past, about what he had gone through during the Holocaust. She had never asked and he had certainly never supplied anything more. But she was a year older now, in high school, and starting to emotionally rebel against her father in every way possible, much to her mom's disappointment and more often, consternation.

"You want me to come to your school and talk about a horrific experience that none of you spoiled brats could ever imagine? Put me on display like I'm some circus animal so they can see this?" pushing up his shirtsleeve to show the blurred blue lines of a serial number that had graced his left forearm now for more than 20 years.

"Sam, she didn't mean anything by it," her mom said soothingly, trying to placate her father and talk him down before he fully erupted.

"No," her father exploded angrily as he stood up abruptly from the table, his chair falling back and crashing to the floor. "The girl thinks because of my experiences during the war, I'm supposed to share them like, what do you say in this country, show and tell? The world let what happened to me, to my family, to all the other six million Jews and did nothing. Nothing," he yelled at Becky. "Don't you dare ever ask me again something so ridiculous," and with that he stormed off, stomping up the stairs as he went to his bedroom and slamming the door behind him so loudly that even the dishes in the kitchen cabinets rattled.

Becky felt sick. So sick over what had just happened she thought that the little contents of her dinner she had managed to eat before the blowup might come back up.

"I'm sorry," Becky said meekly in the form of an apology to her mom.

"Rivka," Judy said coolly now, not taking her eyes off her half-eaten plate of spaghetti. "There are some things you just don't know and will never understand," she started, almost parroting her dad's earlier words. Then finally looking up to fix her daughter with a hardened stare said, "Let the dead rest," in a tone that would have frozen even the warmest of hearts. And then in a tone so soft Becky thought she was imagining it, her mother said again "the dead are resting.

Pittsburgh, Pennsylvania
2006

Thanks to the Internet Becky had stumbled across page after page on the most wanted Nazi war criminals, some of whom had been caught and captured, others who had forever eluded the authorities. Which was fine and all except that these men had all been top-level officials in the Nazi hierarchy. They hadn't just been guards or low-level officers, men whose names would never grace the pages of history books or be portrayed by some famous actor like Gregory Peck as the infamous sadistic doctor Josef Mengele in the 1979 film *The Boys from Brazil.*

But then she stumbled across a 1964 article from *The New York*

Times about the identification of a former Nazi camp guard who was living the life of a housewife in Queens.

"She declared, however, that she had never been more than a guard and had no authority whatever," Becky read to Adam as they sat up together in bed, he reading a book, she from her computer screen.

"Well, of course they'll say that," he replied, his eyes still engrossed on the pages of a book called *Game of Thrones*.

"And get this," Becky continued reading. "I was punished enough. I was in prison three years. Three years, can you imagine? And now they want something again from me?"

"Three years is punishment enough," Adam mimicked with disgust. "From that statement alone, you know she was 'one of them.' Not to mention, some of the camp guards were the most heinous and cruel with their actions towards the prisoners. So to me, as the child of a Holocaust survivor, that statement means shit."

Seeing Becky's pained expression, her lips pursed together, he quickly said, "Hey, you know what I mean. That was against that woman."

"My father is no better," she said, desperately wanting to cry but wanting to show him she was stronger than that. That whoever her father actually was, he wasn't her.

"No, maybe not, but like I said before, you're not him. Never have and never been. I know I never met your mom, but you sound just like her from what you've told me about her. Not to mention, she sounded like a pretty resilient and tough ol' Jew and you, sweetheart, are just that."

"Thanks, babe," Becky said, leaning up to kiss him.

"So whatever happened to this piece of shit, so be it," Adam said, opening up his arms fully now so that Becky could snuggle into his embrace.

"Wow," Becky said as her eyes focused on the new tab she had just opened about the former Hermine Braunsteiner. "She was the first Nazi war criminal to be extradited from the United States to face trial in what was then West Germany."

"When did this happen?" Adam asked.

"She was sent back to Germany in 1973." Continuing to read she said, "The West German government requested her extradition, accusing her of joint responsibility in the deaths of 200,000 people, at Majdanek concentration camp in Poland. 'Stomping Mare' as she was known by the prisoners, was said to have whipped women to death, thrown children by their hair onto trucks that took them to their deaths in gas chambers, hanged young female prisoners and stomped an old woman to-"her voice broke off then, unable to continue to say out loud let alone read the horrors a woman could do to others.

Gently taking her laptop from her, Adam continued to read the article silently to himself but then said out loud, "On June 30, 1981, the court imposed a life sentence, a more severe punishment than those meted out to her co-defendants. Complications of diabetes, including a leg amputation, led to her release from Mülheimer women's prison in 1996. Hermine Braunsteiner Ryan died on April 19, 1999, aged 79, in Bochum, Germany."

"So she basically got to live a full life," Becky said, not really asking but saying this as more of a declarative statement.

"Most of them did babe, as messed up and sad as it is," Adam told her, both of them not acknowledging the elephant in the room that was her father who was still living a full life. He continued to skim the text on the webpage until he added, "Hey, this is interesting, well, good or bad interesting I guess."

"What?" Becky asked, intrigued now by what he had to say.

"After the publicity surrounding Ryan's extradition, the American government in 1979 established a United States Department of Justice Office of Special Investigations to seek out war criminals to denaturalize or deport."

"So, you're telling me I could contact this office, they could technically look into him, into his past and he could lose his American citizenship and be deported?"

"Yes, that's what it seems like," Adam told her, his tone now noncommittal over the enormity of what he had just said out loud to her.

Becky paused then, starting to speak but stopping herself, remembering what Ryan's husband had told reporters in *The New York Times* article from the '60s.

"These people are just swinging axes at random. Didn't they
ever hear the expression, 'Let the dead rest'?"

The dead are resting. Let the dead rest. Two statements uttered around the same time by two totally different people, strangers to each other but tied indirectly together because of the events of the Holocaust. Her mom, a Jewish woman, who, had she lived in Europe during the Second World War would have undoubtedly been killed or imprisoned, as were many of her distant relatives back in Lithuania. And then this man, the husband of a Nazi camp guard who claimed he never knew that the woman he married had once knowingly and willingly killed and tortured Jews.

Her mom, thought Becky, this man, asked the world that was condemning his wife, to 'let the dead rest.' But should they? Should the world truly let the six million dead, 1.5 million of whom were children, let the perpetrators of this ethnic cleansing go free? Should Becky let her father, who was one such perpetrator, never have to pay for his crimes against the Jews, the killing of her people whose blood ran within her?

When Becky woke the next morning, Adam was already gone but next to her filled coffee mug that he sweetly prepared for her each and every morning was a print-out from a newspaper online. He had stapled it but had written the words at the top of the page-

Read the highlighted text first. I'll see you tonight. I love you! -A

"Don't look at these people and say they look frail and weak. Think of someone who at the height of his powers devoted his energies to murdering men, women, and children. The passage of time in no way diminishes the guilt of the killers. Old age should not provide protection. The fact that they have reached an elderly age does not turn them into righteous gentiles."

A chill ran down Becky's spine upon reading these words. She immediately sat down at her laptop and Googled the name "Efraim Zuroff." Scanning his biography she saw that he was an American-born Israeli Nazi hunter who had spent his life bringing Nazi war criminals to trial, many of whom were **living in the United States.**

"Was highlighting that section of text your way of saying I need to contact the Department of Justice about my father?"

Becky had spent all day waiting to say this to Adam but delivered it in a much more confrontational and colder manner than she had intended (or rehearsed in her head).

"What?" Adam sputtered. "What are you talking about?"

"That quote by that Nazi hunter was pretty harsh, not to mention acutely black and white. Are you basically saying to me that if I don't call, you will?"

"Hey Becky, babe, calm down." He got up then from his chair, pulled her out of the chair she was sitting in, only for him to sit back down in it and pull her back onto his lap. "I highlighted it for you. I told you weeks and weeks ago, I play no factor in whatever you decide. I am here solely for you, to support the decision you come to unequivocally. But I know that this is plaguing you to the point you're not sleeping, you pick at your food."

She started to object but he held up his hand, silently asking her to please let him continue.

"I think for many of us, maybe even all of us, we see an elderly person, we see the good they've done the last however many decades, the rich and full lives they've led, and we think, 'they turned their life around, they put all of that behind them, it was a terrible maybe even monstrous thing they did in their youth but it was so long ago, shouldn't we just forget about it?' Me, my personal opinion on the matter is that no, age should not exonerate the person. I think for a lot of innocent crimes perhaps, yes, good behavior should wipe clean a person's slate. But the events of the Holocaust? The orchestrated killing of our people? No, I personally don't think good behavior can ever wipe that slate clean. But, I swear to you on the memory of my father, I won't judge you, I won't hold it against you, think any less of you, if you decide to, as that Nazi woman's husband said in the article, 'let the dead rest.' I will be here with you every step of the way for as long as you want me."

"I can stand so many things in life but I don't think I could stand it if you ever thought less of me, thought me a bad person," Becky said, not able to meet his gaze. And then in a whispered tone she added, "I want you forever."

"Never, that could never happen, babe," he said in such a sure and confident way. "Well, good, because the desired term length of this relationship is mutual." And then he kissed her, once again temporarily assuaging her fears and anxieties where her father, whose fate was in her hands, was concerned.

CHAPTER 16

Pittsburgh, Pennsylvania
2006

"I want you to meet my mom," Adam said to her as they walked along Murray Avenue, having just come from the Manor theater where they had caught an Iranian movie.

"What?" Becky stopped abruptly, pulling her hand from his, their fingers having been intertwined only moments before.

"We've been going out for more than half a year, I don't think it's so crazy an idea for me to want you to meet my closest living relative," he told her almost sheepishly.

"It's not that," she began, turning away from him to look down the side street at the row of identical houses, all mirror images of the one she had grown up in.

"Then what is it?" Adam asked, his tone conveying a growing trace of annoyance.

Still not looking at him but in a tone loud enough she knew he'd hear it, she said, "Because of who she is and who I am."

"You're you. You weren't alive in the 1940s, you weren't in the ghettos, the camps. You have nothing to do with what your father did."

"His blood runs within me."

"Yes, and so does the blood of your Jewish ancestors. Why is it that you seem to forget or deliberately omit that part constantly during your mental mind games you keep playing with yourself?"

She had no answer so she couldn't reply. Because everything he had just said was true.

"Meet her," he said, his words coming out as almost a demand. But then added, "please...for me."

"And if I truly can't bring myself to?" she said to him, finally turning back around.

"Then I don't think we have a future anymore," he replied in a tone devoid of any feeling or emotion, coldness being the only thing that resonated from him. And with that, he walked back towards his parked car, leaving her to stare after him.

⚜

When he started driving towards Bloomfield and not towards Shadyside where he lived, she knew he was taking her home. That they would not be spending the evening together as they usually did.

A pit started to form in Becky's stomach as she got out of Adam's car. He didn't look or say anything to her, instead just stared straight out, his hands on the wheel. As soon as the car door was shut, he drove off without so much as a backward glance or wave.

"So that's that," Becky thought to herself as she walked inside her building, feeling almost if not more dejected than when Danny told her he wanted a divorce. Danny's bombshell had hurt her deeply at the time but she knew they had grown apart during the years of their marriage, each of them wanting different things out of life. With Adam she was years older and wiser, any girlhood infatuation of being married and having a husband replaced by the fact that she loved him and truly could see how great a friend and lover he was, a true partner in every way. Even

114

if she never married again because truly, that didn't really matter to her, she didn't want to lose what she had with him.

Becky wasn't one for believing in kismet. And yet as she sat in her window alcove (one of the main reasons she had taken the apartment), a cup of lavender Earl Grey tea between her hands, she thought back that perhaps almost everything in the last year HAD happened for a reason.

The circumstances in which she and Adam had met weren't ideal or romantic or anything to gush about when telling strangers in years to come, but something had drawn both her and Adam together to start attending the Second Generation Group at the same time. And that day that Adam just happened to be on Liberty Avenue the same time she was coming out of Donatelli's?

But then Becky thought back to her chance encounter with Ursula in Berlin. A Holocaust survivor who spoke perfect English, who somehow knew she was Jewish even though until then, every other German she had encountered seemed to take her for a native non-Jewish German. How it was Ursula who told her about the *Topographie des Terrors* and how by going there, she had discovered her father's dark secret past that had remained buried for so long.

Picking up her cell phone, she tapped on the icon, then recent, and then pushed the one that said "Adam."

The phone rang and rang, and fearing he was deliberately avoiding her, she was about to admit defeat and hang up when he answered, although the line remained quiet.

Knowing he was waiting for her to speak, to say something, she said, "I'm sorry. And if you haven't given up on me, yes, I would very much like to meet your mom. Meet the woman responsible for raising such a wonderful man."

"I think that can be arranged," he said playfully. And just like that, the horrible pit that had formed in Becky's stomach was gone, almost as if something had just pressed a button that said "release."

⚜ CHAPTER 17 ⚜

Pittsburgh, Pennsylvania
2006

"Come in, come in," Adam's mom Minah said in heavily accented English as she ushered them inside. Taking Becky's hands within her own aged and gnarled ones, she said, "I am so happy to finally meet this Becky, this woman my *meshuggener* of a son keeps going on and on about. Although I won't lie, for a while, I thought perhaps you were made up, how do you say it, not real. Yes?" Her dark brown eyes were twinkling with pure delight.

"Ma, hey now, be good," Adam told her jokingly, "or we're out of here."

"Not before you eat all my macaroons," she answered just as he was about to put one into his mouth. Turning to Becky she said, "See? I'm good for something," and they all laughed.

His mouth somewhat full Adam said, "Ma always made the best macaroons. Not an easy feat considering all my classmates also had moms who all thought themselves the best macaroon makers this side of the Pale of Settlement."

"Where did you go to school?" Becky asked rather abruptly, but curious now that he mentioned it as the subject had never come up before.

"The Hillel Academy. Being the eldest son, my parents hoped that I'd become a rabbi, do my grandfather proud-"

"My father was an esteemed rabbinical scholar back in our town," his mom interjected, proudly stating this to Becky.

Continuing on he said, "Thankfully, my younger brother willingly and gladly filled the Judaica shoes of the family which let me off the hook to pursue my passion for law. But not that I don't remember every painstaking, minute detail of the Talmud since I had to study it for hours each day for 12 years straight," as he plopped a second macaroon into his mouth.

"Oh you bad bad boy," his mom lightly swatted at him as he engulfed this tiny, not even five foot tall woman into his arms.

Becky stared in amazement at the scene before her. Prior to coming here she wasn't sure what his mom would be like. She knew from what Adam had mentioned before, both at the Second Generation meetings and privately, that she had never been shy about her experiences during the war. That she had never wanted to keep them hidden, locked in the painful recesses of the past, unlike her father. That for decades and even to this day she went to local schools to talk about the Holocaust. Looking at this tiny, elderly woman now, never would anyone believe that she had survived for years in a living hell like Auschwitz, that she had survived a pogrom that took place AFTER the war had ended, when so many people thought they were a thing of Czarist Russia and not post-war Europe. But even with all that she had endured, all the losses she had suffered, Becky could tell that never once in her life did she take her survival for granted.

"So Adam tells me you met at the JCC, in the gym? I have to say, that's so modern, almost like out of some movie," his mom said.

Becky looked at Adam with quizzical eyes, but he just looked back at her with a look that said "trust me." So going along with it she replied, "Yes. My very own Prince Charming who was at the treadmill right next to me."

His mom had started leading them towards the dining room but not before stopping at the baby grand piano that was adorned with an antique looking white shawl and topped with black and white photographs. Seeing Becky stare at the photographs Minah said, "My own avenue of the dead. My entire family was killed in the Holocaust, you know. We were a family of ten and I am the only survivor to say *Kaddish* after them."

"If you don't mind me asking, how did your pictures survive?" Becky asked Minah tentatively, hoping she wouldn't upset her nor Adam for asking about a sensitive topic, especially since Adam hadn't told her the true circumstances of how they had met.

"Survive the war you mean?" she replied, slowly taking a sip of her coffee.

"Yes," Becky said. "Um, I know, I mean I've spoken with some survivors who said they didn't even have a photo of their parents or brothers or sisters or husband or wife." She was thinking of her father and the lie he had perpetuated all those years that he had been able to keep nothing from his life before he was deported to Auschwitz.

"Many of the Gentiles in my town, people who we Jews had happily lived side by side with for decades, turned on us overnight. The men were the worst. After the Germans invaded you see, they enlisted men into the police. Never were there such loyal and eager collaborators as these men. Men who only weeks, months, a mere year before who you had spoken with, purchased goods from, became the same men who laughed and mocked hilariously when the Germans slashed the beards and cut off the sidelocks of the most devout men. Who took our homes and our belongings when we were forced into the ghetto."

Becky felt trapped, unsure if she should apologize to Minah, telling her she didn't need continue recounting this painful part of her past but wanting to hear more all the same. Wanting to hear from an actual survivor. So she remained silent, letting Minah continue.

"But even during the darkest days in Kielce, before the town was *Judenfrei*, there remained a few good Gentiles. An elderly woman, in particular, who out of pity for how poor she was, my mother would sometimes pay to have her help with the laundry and the house cleaning, she often smuggled stale bread and rotten vegetables into the ghetto for us. The last time I saw her before we were sent to the camp, I gave her all my photographs. When we were forced from our home, I had removed all the photographs from their frames and put them inside my brassiere. I wore them on me every moment of the day we were in the ghetto. But I knew that wherever they were sending us, my pictures wouldn't be safe anymore. So I gave them to Jadwiga that night. She told me she would guard them with her life. And she did. After the war, I found her and she still had them. Like so many innocent Poles, she had become homeless during the war, endured starvation, but she never let go of my pictures, she never once let go of the only ties I would ever have of my murdered family. And I'm so glad she didn't. Because if I hadn't given them to her, my pictures of my dead family would have been thrown in the mud like so many others had happen to them when they arrived at Auschwitz, their former lives forever ripped from them the moment they stepped foot on those tracks."

"Before you say anything, I only lied about how we met, not because I feel different or ashamed even about your father, but because I wanted to leave everything up to you. What you do or do not want to say, what you feel comfortable with-"

Becky cut off Adam by putting her index finger over his lips and just said, "Shh. It's okay. I'm glad you did."

"You are?" he asked with a tone of surprise in his voice.

"Yes. I'm glad tonight could just be about meeting your mom and have nothing to do with my father or me. And besides, I truly don't think I've ever met a more incredible or heroic woman."

"She is that," he said proudly. "Although being modest and the somewhat stubborn woman that she is, she'd probably disagree with your assessment of her and tell you she's an ordinary person like anyone else with the same aches and pains as every other elderly person out there but she really is. I know there are many other survivors like her, what they endured, but…"

His voice breaking with emotion, Becky finished the sentence, "but she's YOUR incredible mother," as she lightly kissed him on the cheek. He smiled at her then, a warm, rich smile with so much meaning, put the car into gear and started off for home.

CHAPTER 18

Pittsburgh, Pennsylvania
2006

"Do you forgive them?"

After their initial meeting, Adam's mom called Becky the following week, inviting her to tea. Too surprised and caught off guard by the invitation to say anything else, she had accepted. Nervous about going, about spending time with his mom alone, she was immediately put at ease when Minah (as she insisted Becky call her) took her hand and led her to the dining room table. There before her was a scene that made Becky think of one of her favorite books from childhood, *The Secret Garden.* She half expected to see the characters of Mary Lennox, Martha and her brother Dickon, and of course Colin appear at any moment for how lovely and how very British everything looked, like it was from another time. Minah revealed to Becky that growing up in her small town in Poland before the war, she had desperately wanted to go to England, to be British in fact, and that her most prized possession as a child had been a porcelain doll-size tea set an over-indulgent and doting grandfather had bought her for her eighth birthday after bartering with a traveling peddler.

Minah didn't drive anymore so Becky had come to her house again, although this time she had brought with her refreshments, freshly baked *sfogliatelle* she had picked up earlier that morning, which the women enjoyed with cups of coffee. A light dusting of crumbs on the plates were all that remained of the delectable orange flavored Italian pastry which both of them had greedily devoured. Becky wasn't planning on "going there," on talking about the past, a past tied to her, but the words were out of her mouth before she could stop them.

"Yes."

Becky hadn't said whom she was referring to when she asked if Minah forgave them, but Minah knew. Minah knew exactly what Becky was talking about.

"Why?" Becky asked, a slight note of pain in her voice. "After all that happened, all that you went through, I mean, the loss of your ENTIRE family, how could you ever forgive the people who did that?"

"Because forgiveness doesn't mean I could ever forget-forget what happened to my family, to my home, to my people, forget what I went through. But not forgiving, it would have just led to more hatred in my heart, hatred that would have grown into something bigger, ruining my life, but also ruining the life of my children who were born from the ashes from the death and destruction I endured. My girl, trust me when I say I've known too many survivors who were never able to leave behind the camps, the ghettos. They physically survived, but mentally, emotionally, their hearts and souls died all those years ago."

There was silence then, neither woman speaking.

"Something is troubling you," Minah said, saying this not as a question but rather as a statement. "I could tell from the first time we met, although I don't think it has anything to do with my son, with your relationship with him."

"No, not at all," Becky quickly said. "He's the best thing that's happened to me in a very long time."

"But it has to do with the war, with the Holocaust?"

My God, was the woman a clairvoyant, Becky thought?

For Minah, Becky's silence acted as confirmation to her question.

"Adam told me your mother was born here."

"Yes, my grandparents and my aunts and uncles came to Pittsburgh, to America, in the 1920s. From a region in Lithuania."

"And your father was German?"

Becky once again let her silence serve as her answer to the question.

"There was a man in my town who went to university in Germany. A fellow Jew. He was one of the few people we knew who had a wireless. I'll always remember one night being at his house with my parents and hearing Hitler's voice for the first time. How he shouted, he sounded almost hysterical, screaming things like Jews were why Germany had lost the war, that we had stabbed Germany in the back, that we were nothing but dirty capitalists and that we were part of the threat to the world. After his speech ended, the man turned off the wireless and we all said nothing. We readied ourselves to go and he said, 'It will never happen here. Hitler is just an unpleasantness that will fade away. Not in Germany. *Nicht in Deutschland.*' And even after the Nazis took his wife and child away in a cattle car in the first action, this same man still didn't believe that the Germans meant to completely wipe our people from the face of the earth." She paused then before adding, "He killed himself in the ghetto. People said he was trying to escape but escape to what, to where? I think he was just looking for a quick way to die."

"My father grew up in Berlin," Becky began tentatively. "An unobservant Jew was how he always referred to his childhood. He was, is, much more observant and devout here, the man I've always known. He had a small family, but he was the only survivor. He's not an easy man to understand, to like even. My relationship with him has always been strained. I just thought this had to do with his experiences during the war, with survivor's guilt. But lately, stuff has happened, where...-"she trailed off, unable to finish. Taking a deep breath, she finished, "where I don't think he's the man he says he is."

An awkward, even uncomfortable silence descended upon the room then. Becky wished Minah would say something, anything, but the older woman remained quiet.

"Have you been able to prove your assumptions? To obtain some sort of proof?" Minah quietly asked.

Becky thought of the black and white photograph she had seen on a rainy, cold night in Berlin which had haunted her ever since. "Yes," she answered.

"Only you can ultimately decide what to do. These Nazi hunters, the Wiesenthals of the world, I think to myself, yes, there is good in what they're doing. Capturing former officials, guards, to some survivors, their descendants, this helps in bringing closure. To others, it opens up old wounds that had closed but never fully healed. For me personally, remembering, never forgetting the stories of both the survivors and the dead, is what I want most. Not highly public trials that become more of a, how do you say it, 'media circus?' yes? than anything else."

Unsure if she had the right to even say this, Becky tentatively began, "People always said about the Nazis, what rights did they have to play God, to decide who lived and who died? Aren't I doing the same thing with the fate of my father?"

Coming over to sit next to Becky on the worn and weathered loveseat, Minah took Becky's clammy hands in her own gnarled ones and said, "No, my dear. We Jews, we did nothing to deserve what the Nazis did to us, so no, they had no right to 'play God' as you called it.

Your father, he alone, chose the path he did. That is the difference."

And just like that, Becky's mind was made up.

The following week when she dropped off the groceries at her father's house, she deliberately went when she knew he wouldn't be there. Every Tuesday morning at 10 he walked the short distance to the library, spending roughly an hour or so there perusing the stacks, finding two new books to take home and read for that week. It had been his custom since he had retired.

After getting everything put away, she retrieved her purse from the living room and took out two things. The first, a 4 x 6 reprint of the photo, THAT photo, and second, her mom's tiny frayed black notebook.

She left them both on the kitchen table, both articles propped up against a vase of artificial flowers that hadn't been changed out to something else since her mom had been alive. And as she closed and locked the back door behind her, through the windowpane, she could see her father's younger self staring back at her.

And then she waited for the phone call.

⚜ CHAPTER 19 ⚜

Pittsburgh, Pennsylvania
2006

"You think you're so clever, leaving these things and then running off like some childish coward, not even having the decency to face me as a grown woman?"

Sam's harsh words after she had mumbled a groggy hello into the receiver quickly jolted her awake even though the clock said it was almost 2 AM. She had spent all day waiting, expecting him to call her, to demand to know what sort of games she was playing, to even deny everything. But no call ever came and so she went to bed around 10PM and slept until the phone rang hours later, waking her from a deep slumber.

"I had every intention of facing you," Becky calmly said, refusing to be baited by him, to let him get control of the situation in which she knew she clearly had the upper hand. "But it's 2 in the morning and I'm not having this talk now on the phone. I will come to your house tomorrow after work," and before he could say anything else, she hung up on him, her hands shaking as she did.

She waited anxiously for a minute or two, fearing the phone would ring again, he being even more indignant now over her hanging up on him, but nothing. She removed the pillow her head had been resting on, placed it over her mouth and let out a muffled scream. She then replaced the pillow to rest behind her head once more, closing her eyes, only to immediately re-open them, knowing that there was no way whatsoever she'd be able to fall back asleep for the next four hours until her alarm went off. Not to mention doubting she'd be able to get any work done tomorrow either.

As Becky knew it would, the next day at work passed by interminably, painfully slow and not without its share of mishaps. There was no one home at two of her three scheduled home visits for that day; she spilled coffee all over herself once she got to the office only to discover in sheer mortification that she had forgotten to put on a cami underneath her very sheer blouse; and in the course of an hour, had managed to ream out both her department's secretary and intern, which in hindsight was a gross overreaction on her part. And all of this before lunch.

She stopped at her apartment before heading to her father's house, changing into a fresh top and touching up her makeup, trying to mask the dark circles beneath her eyes which she was loath to admit made her look a lot older than she was. But they had been there, a now worn and haggard look on her face ever since she had gotten back from Germany.

When she got to Sam's house, Becky briefly considered knocking, as if the house she had grown up in as a child was now that of a stranger. But wasn't it in some way? Wasn't everything about her father now akin to him being a stranger to her? At the last second she thought better of it and rummaged around in her purse for the key.

She drew up short upon entering to see her father sitting in his usual chair, which he had moved to face the front door, a glass of, she presumed, brandy in his left hand, as if he was ready to pounce. Had he been like that ever since she had hung up on him, she wondered.

Becky paused, considering what to say, no, rather how to begin when her father quietly but with a trace of steel hardness said, "how did you know?"

So he wasn't denying it, she thought. He wasn't denying that it was him in the photo, him dressed in a SS uniform, laughing all the while, posing at the most heinous place to have existed during the Holocaust.

"Your wedding portrait," she replied.

Becky knew he knew that she had a card she hadn't played when she left the copy of the picture and her mom's notebook on the kitchen table. Had only those two things existed, he could have perhaps gotten away with it, denied it and claimed it wasn't him in the picture, just an uncanny resemblance to someone else who was posing on that summer day mere miles from where people like Minah and her family and perhaps even distant relatives of her mom were being gassed and worked to death. But the wedding portrait was his sinker and they both knew it.

There were so many things Becky wanted to say to him. But she said the one thing for the one person who wasn't there now to say for herself. "How could you do that to mom?"

"Your mother," he began, throwing back the remainder of the contents in his glass. "She was lucky to have me. I can't say the same about her. Me, a true member of the Aryan race, marrying not only a dirty Jew, but a cripple at that. Your mother is the reason why the T4 program was started. *Lebensunwertes Leben*, 'life unworthy of life'. You've been a disappointment to me your entire life, Rivka,"- saying her Hebrew name in a long, drawn out sneer, "but at least you inherited your Aryan genes."

As this vile rhetoric spewed from his mouth, Becky stared back at him in horror and revulsion. Her mind was spinning, no, spiraling out of control but she was still cognizant enough to ask, "What was T4?"

"*Rassenhygiene.* Racial hygiene. A program designed to eliminate from the chain of heredity, anyone mentally or physically **unworthy**. A way to ensure that the German people would never again be tainted by dysgenics."

At the mention of dysgenics, the infusion of degenerate elements into the bloodstream, Becky immediately flashed back to one of her earliest social work classes, describing how the eugenics movement in the United States had taken root during the 1920s and '30s and how the state of California had subjected more people to forced sterilizations than all of the other United States combined.

"You're telling me mom would have been sterilized…or worse, simply because an illness from childhood left her physically disabled? A disease that had nothing to do at all with genetics?" Becky asked incredulously, her voice rising as she said this.

"*Lebensunwertes Leben,* life unworthy of life," was all he said with an eerie degree of calmness, the raving man from the phone in the middle of the night nothing more than a figment of her imagination. The man before her like every Nazi she had ever seen or heard about, denying they had done anything wrong, claiming it had all been for the good of mankind, but only the mankind they advocated for.

"What was your name? Your real name?" she asked.

"Max von Hofmannsthal. But he died the night I killed my good old friend Samuel Weiss from Berlin and became a dirty Jew. The night **I** became Samuel Weiss."

Part II

Sam & Max

❧ CHAPTER 20 ❧

Berlin, Germany
February 27, 1933

"When we're older, Marta and I will marry. And then we'll truly be brothers," Max said to his best friend Sam as they made their way home from school, cutting through the Tiergarten, their preferred route. Friends since before birth (their pregnant mothers had met on the day Max's parents moved into the apartment on *Kroenstraße,* one floor up from Sam's parents), they spent every waking moment together, each boy as constant and steady a fixture at the other boy's apartment as he was in his own home.

"What??" Sam sputtered, a look of incredulity passing across his face as he stopped dead in his tracks in the midst of Berlin's beloved park. "Trust me Max, you don't want to marry her, or any girl. But especially not Marta," he said with such a tone of derision that it almost made Max laugh to hear Sam talk about his younger sister that way. Although Sam was the older of the two boys by nearly two months, Max had become obsessed with the opposite sex lately and seemed to talk of very little else. The boys were only 12 and Sam didn't want to be thinking about marrying and growing up, not with topics like Adolf Hitler and his Nazis causing so much concern and

133

hushed talk amongst the grownups.

"Marta knows me, I know Marta, and my *mutti* just adores her. She'd finally get the daughter she always wanted." After Max, she had given birth to three other babies, all girls, all stillborn. It was a grief she had never fully recovered from, causing a break in her marriage to Max's father that had never been and never would fully be repaired. But it was true about Marta. She was the one person whose company Max's mother seemed to really enjoy.

Wanting to change the subject, anything to not talk about Max and Marta getting married, Sam asked, "So you want to go to the pictures this weekend?" Max hadn't replied, so lightly elbowing him he said, *"Maximilian,"* calling Max by his full name, something he knew the other boy hated.

"I wonder why there's so many storm troopers out today," Max mused as they continued walking in the direction of the Reichstag, home of the German parliament.

Sam had, of course, also noticed the larger than usual number of storm troopers, or Brownshirts as the papers sometimes referred to them due to the brown shirts they wore, and wondered the same thing himself. But he had opted to ignore them, hoping that by doing so, they'd go away. Not just now but completely from the streets of Berlin and the rest of Germany, where their often harassing and threatening behavior was completely unchecked, especially now in the month since *Herr* Hitler had been sworn in as Chancellor of Germany.

But now, with Max's attention entirely focused on the storm troopers and nothing else, Sam started to feel uneasy, immediately regretting having stopped at Café Kranzler for a hot chocolate and strudel instead of going straight home.

"Come on Max, it will be dark soon," Sam said, starting to pull on the other boy's sleeve.

"You go on ahead," Max said, his eyes still focused on the large group of storm troopers that were congregating together around a nearby park bench. "I'm going to stick around and see what's going on."

In a Germany before Jews had become "enemies of the German people," as Adolf Hitler liked to put it, or unwittingly become the scapegoats as to the real reason why Germany had been humiliatingly defeated in the Great War 15 years earlier, Sam would have stayed. Because that Sam, the Sam from before Adolf Hitler, would have been just as curious as Max as to what was going on. But the Sam of now, the dark-haired boy of 12 who was the exact physical opposite of his blond-haired and blue eyed friend, knew he should leave. For where there were storm troopers, he knew the streets wouldn't be safe for a Jew like him, child or not.

The moment Sam stepped inside his family's apartment, his parents immediately stopped talking and just stared at him for a moment-his father's look one of annoyance, even anger, his mother's one of deep concern and worry. It was her face that made Sam regret once more not having come right home after school.

And then before he knew what was happening, his father stomped over to him and hit him on the back of his head. "Where were you? You had your *mutti* sick with worry. And in these times, to be out on the streets alone when it's nearing dark," he yelled at Sam.

"Benjamin, enough," Sam's mother quietly commanded. "The boy is home now, he's safe, everything is fine." And then to Sam she said, "Go wash up *libeling*, Katja is almost ready with dinner."

Sam left in the direction of the washroom, glad his mother had intervened and been able to pacify his father, at least for now. His father seemed to do nothing but worry anymore and on more than one occasion had said they should leave Germany, to which each time his mother had laughed outrageously and even called his father absurd for suggesting such an idea.

"Where have you been? You know, your schoolboy antics are causing a lot of fights between *Vati* and *Mutti* lately," his sister Marta said haughtily, in that too often goody two shoes way of hers.

"Well, I am a schoolboy so I guess that shouldn't come as too much of a surprise to them," Sam fired back. He was older than her by nearly two years and yet she often behaved like she was the older sibling. And then, knowing that this would really annoy her, he said, "Max told me tonight that you and he are going to get married when you're older." He said this as a joke, as a way of being funny and lightening the tense mood throughout the apartment but he wasn't prepared for his sister's harsh reaction.

"Like I'd ever marry a Nazi. What a vile thing to say," Marta told him disgustedly.

"Max isn't a Nazi," Sam said immediately in defense of his friend.

"Oh yeah?" Marta replied. "What do you think the *Deutsches Jungvolk in der Hitler Jugend* is?" She was referring to the division of the Hitler Youth organization that was specifically for boys between the ages of 10-14. "Nazis in the making," she continued. "In two years he'll join the Hitler Youth proper and then in due time become one of them," saying the last word like how someone would react to having to get a tooth pulled at the dentist. "And besides, *Herr* von Hofmannsthal is one of the biggest Nazi supporters of them all."

That Sam couldn't deny. He hated going to Max's apartment anymore to play, given how much the inside looked like a Nazi party rally, what with its numerous swastika flags adorning various rooms and then a massive portrait of Hitler himself hanging over the fireplace, his beady eyes seeming to follow you no matter where you went.

Taking a softer tone, Marta came to stand by him so that they were both looking into the mirror now. "Sam, you really need to be paying attention more to what's going on around you. You're no longer a child. I know *Mutti* denies it but *Vati* is worried that stuff is going to get really bad for us Jews here. And I believe him. And you should too."

When Sam entered the breakfast room the following morning, everyone's faces were ashen, no one was saying a word. He stole a look at *The Berliner Tageblatt*, Father's preferred newspaper, and immediately felt nauseous when he read the front page headlines-

"Reichstag destroyed by arson, Communists to blame!"

"President Hindenburg invoking Article 48"

"Cabinet members drawing up 'Decree of the Reich President for the Protection of the People State"

"*Vati*? What does this mean?" Sam asked his father, his voice sounding like that of a small child who desperately wanted reassurance that everything was going to be okay.

"It means, my boy," Sam's father began, "that the Germany I fought for during the war, the Germany that I gladly took a bullet and shrapnel for," slapping his palm down hard on his injured leg, "is no more!"

The room was left in stunned silence until a moment later, his father roughly pushed his chair back on the wooden floor, the sound he knew would irritate *Mutti*, and stormed from the room.

"The act is abolishing freedom of speech, assembly, privacy, and the press," Marta whispered to him from across the table. "Even phone tapping is going to be legal."

"That's enough children. Eat your breakfast and finish getting ready for school," *Mutti* said half-dazed, even though it appeared that she herself hadn't touched anything on her plate. Her fingertips were wrapped so tightly around the edge of her coffee cup, they looked as white as the walls in the room. She didn't drink anything from it. Rather, it seemed to Sam that if she were to loosen her grip on the cup, the chaos that now reigned outside would somehow invade their home…

"The sooner Germany is rid of the Communist and Jew filth, the better," Max's father said, as he closed the pages of the *The Völkischer Beobachter*, the newspaper of the Nazi party, not before adjusting the swastika pin he proudly wore on the lapel of his suit jacket.

"You don't mean Sam though? And Marta, right *Vater*?" Max asked. "I mean, they're good Jews. And they're German. I mean *Herr* Weiss was injured fighting for Germany during the war."

"Hildegard, I thought I told you I didn't want the boy playing with that Jew anymore." Max's father said this to his mother, as if he wasn't even in the room at all. For as long as he could remember, he had always been "the boy." Never "Max" or even "son." Just "the boy." He had vowed a long time ago to not let his father's dismissal of him bother him, but it still pained him to hear it.

"And I told you many times that Giselle Weiss is a good friend of mine and her son is your own child's best friend, lest you forget that. It's not as if he was ever over abundantly blessed in that department."

His mother was referring to the difficult time Max had making friends. When he was younger most of it had to do with the fact that Max suffered from a terrible stutter which had caused him to be mercilessly taunted at school when Sam wasn't around to defend him and on more than one occasion, fight the bully. And even when he grew out of it by the age of 7, Max was still extremely shy. Sam and his sister Marta were the only children his own age he felt completely comfortable with. Max knew his mother hadn't said it to be mean but his lack of popularity, and his even greater lack of enthusiasm for the Hitler Youth were just two of the many reasons why he was a disappointment in his father's eyes and why he had always been "the boy."

"I'm not one of your employees at the Reichsbahn, Wilhelm," his mother continued now in a sparring tone. "So find someone else to order around."

And just like that, without missing a beat, Max's mother returned to buffing her flawlessly manicured nails. And just as *Herr* Weiss had stormed from the room in the apartment below, *Herr* von Hofmannsthal did the same, albeit for different reasons.

April 1, 1933

Deutsche! Wehrt Euch! Kauft nicht bei Juden!
Die Juden sind unser Unglück!

It wasn't the sight of the angry and intimidating storm troopers standing outside of the main entrance of the Kaufhaus Nathan Israel department store that caught Sam's attention. A menacing fixture on the capital's streets, Sam was accustomed to seeing these worshipers of Hitler nowadays. Today, however, was an entirely new sight, for it was the message on the placards that they held which alarmed Sam- "Germans, defend yourselves! Don't buy from Jews" and "Jews are our misfortune."

"*Vati,* what does this mean? Why are they doing this?"

Benjamin didn't answer him. He didn't say anything but looked simply crestfallen at this latest form of degradation and humiliation that was being unwillingly heaped upon the Jewish people.

"What are you standing there and waiting for *Jude*? This is the store of YOUR people," one of the storm troopers tauntingly said, adding extra emphasis on the word 'your.'

"Not that they'll be stealing from the German people much longer," another of the storm troopers muttered, which made the whole group laugh as if they were privy to some inside joke.

And with all the emotional strength and dignity he could muster when he felt so beaten to his very core every single day since Hitler had come to power, Benjamin said, "Come along Samuel," and in they went, into one of Berlin's oldest and most prestigious department stores, whose owner was in fact a Jew.

When Sam and his father returned home to their apartment hours later, each one laden with bags bulging with goods that bore the insignia of Kaufhaus Nathan Israel, Sam's mother said, "What's all this?" to which his father dismissively said, "Because I wanted to." And the matter was dropped, the surprising curtness of his father's tone allowing for no further discussion.

It wasn't until that evening when everyone had retired to their bedrooms that Sam heard the knob of his bedroom door slowly turning. He looked up from the book he was reading, an English language copy of *Lord of the Rings* his father had gifted him after his last trip to London, and saw Marta enter, quietly shutting the door behind her.

"All right, tell me the truth," Marta said. "What was the real story behind *Vati* spending hundreds of *Reichsmarks* today on gifts like it was someone's birthday. And then, forbidding me from attending Mila's party at *Café Wien* today."

Sam took a deep breath, desperately wishing his sister would just leave him alone, but wanting even more for the characters of Frodo and Gandalf to be real and not just make-believe. If people like Hitler and the Nazis were real, why couldn't Middle-earth come to life too? But seeing that Marta wasn't going anywhere he said, "Jewish businesses were being boycotted today."

"What?" Marta gasped in disbelief.

"*Vati* bought all that he did I guess out of defiance? Or support of the Israels? I don't know."

"But boycotted how?" Marta persisted.

"Storm troopers were all over the city, standing outside of Jewish owned businesses and shops holding up signs with messages like 'Don't buy from Jews,' 'The Jews are our misfortune,' and 'Go to Palestine.' This whole business, it's breaking Father's spirit."

"But surely *Vati* agreed with the Palestine sign?" Marta sarcastically added. It was no secret within the family that ever since their father's sister *Tante* Rebekah had immigrated to Palestine five years ago and sent them snapshots of her exotic life on a *kibbutz* there, their father had dreamt about immigrating there himself. It was their sophisticated, urbanite mother who had and continued to squash any illusion of the family becoming camel farmers, as she called it.

"That wasn't even the worst part though," Sam said, staring down at the words on the pages of his open book, feeling so distracted and consumed by everything. In almost a whisper he added, "They were making the owners, employees, paint the Star of David in yellow and black on the doors and windows. So there would be absolutely no confusion as to what was and was not a Jewish store."

"I don't know about you, but I think I'd make a pretty good camel farmer," Marta quipped, which made Sam smile and then start to really laugh, the first time he had done so all day.

⚜ CHAPTER 21 ⚜

Berlin, Germany
September 1935

"So I guess the wedding is off."

Sam had said this as a joke, in reference to Max's declaration from a few years earlier that he would one day marry Marta. But Max said nothing, just continuing to stare morosely off into the distance, the mood in the air as thick and depressing as when news first broke about the creation of the Nuremberg Laws, three new laws that reduced the rights of German Jews even further. "If that was even possible," were his father's exact words.

One of the laws now forbade marriages and any intimate extramarital relations between Jews and non-Jewish German citizens. After his father had finished reading the descriptions for each of the new laws, Marta had dryly said, "So what's next, ghettos? Herd us Jews off to live in a restricted area like they did 500 years ago? I mean, they already made it so non-Jews can no longer buy from us."

Since the attack on the Reichstag two years prior and then the death of President von Hindenberg the very next year, resulting in Hitler's combining his position as Chancellor with that of President, essentially making himself the supreme leader of the country, the two lifelong friends saw very little of each other anymore save for when they were at school. They no longer walked to and fro the *Berlinisches Gymnasium* every day like they once had. Sam was always already at school by the time Max got there and hurriedly left the building at the end of each day, never waiting for Max like he once had. Max knew this was to avoid having to be around the other boys and avoid bearing the brunt of their taunts and cruelty when not in the presence of the teachers.

Although he had missed Sam in the beginning, now that he was 14, Max was a proper member of the Hitler Youth, having graduated beyond the German Youngsters, which was for the younger boys. He didn't overly love or believe all of the fiery rhetoric and Nazi party doctrines they were forced to repeat back as if they were parrots, but he did like finally feeling like he belonged somewhere, that he was truly a part of something. And it didn't hurt either that the other boys seemed to like him now, although he knew a lot of that had to do with the fact that his father was a high-ranking member in the Nazi Party. Even his father seemed to tolerate him more now too, actually engaging with him at dinner, asking what had been discussed at that week's Hitler Youth meeting.

Sam had, of course, noticed Max's absence from school the previous week. He had thought about going to his apartment and asking if he was okay but thought better of it, too fearful that it would be *Herr* von Hofmannsthal who would answer the door and not kind *Frau* von Hofmannsthal. But then he had noticed the absence of other boys from their class, boys who proudly wore their Hitler Youth uniforms on meeting days and figured it had something to do with that. It was only after news broke about the rally, the annual event that the radio said was being called "*Reichsparteitag der Freiheit*" or "Freedom Rally" for it "liberated" Germany from the Treaty of Versailles as compulsory military service was reintroduced, something that had been forbidden for 16 years, that Sam knew Max must have been in Nuremberg, at the rally with his father along with the tens of thousands of other fervent Nazis who were in attendance.

But Sam couldn't help himself and before he knew it he was asking, "How can you be a part of something that hates me?" And then taking a deep breath said, "hates all people like me?" his voice straining as he uttered it.

"Don't be silly, Sam," Max said, casually and indifferently Sam felt, as he quickly brushed aside Sam's words. "It's not like that."

"But Max, it is!" Sam rebutted his old friend strongly. "How can you not see it? How can you be so blind to see what the Nazis are doing, have been doing for years now, to the Jews? To anyone who is not the perfect blond hair, blue eyed, Christian specimen?"

Going to stand in front of Max, Sam said almost in anguish, "Max, they're arresting people for no just cause. They're beating innocent people on the street for sport. They're doing this to Germans, innocent people like my father whose family has been here since the 16th century!"

"But you're not German, Sam. You're just a Jew."

Max hadn't meant it as anything cruel, but rather as a reminder to his former friend of his place, of where he truly stood in today's world. But the look of hurt, even shock on Sam's face after he had said it, made Max think for a moment that perhaps he had gone too far. But after the other boy had walked away dejectedly, Max knew that it had needed to be said.

He was discovering that Jews like Sam were the worst, the kind who thought they were just Germans and that Judaism was just their religion like Christianity was his. No, as Max learned, Judaism was their nationality. They were not real Germans, no matter how long they claimed to have been "here."

Max didn't necessarily support the acts of violence against the Jews, unless they deserved it. But he kept these thoughts and opinions to himself when at meetings or talking with his father, which he seemed to do a lot as of late. No, he was simply for the removal of the Jews from all German lands. He knew that they were the reason Germany had lost the war, why hardworking men like the fathers of his friends Gereon and Oberst were unable to find steady work, why Germany had been so humiliated with the terms of the Treaty of Versailles. Once Germany purged itself of the filthy Jews, Max knew Germany would once more return to the majestic heights it had occupied for centuries. He was determined to not only be part of it, but to be there when it happened too.

❧ CHAPTER 22 ❧

Berlin, Germany
November 8, 1938

It was the sound of his parents arguing that woke Sam. They had always disagreed with each other; in fact, his father had once joked that disagreements were a necessary part of marriage, to which his mother had shot him a non-bemused look. But lately their disagreements seemed to have evolved into something else entirely-almost daily fights.

Sam crept to his door and quietly held it ajar so he could hear what they were saying. He was momentarily startled to see Marta doing the same but she just put a finger to her lips indicating to him to not say anything.

"I begged you to leave for Palestine when we had the chance, Giselle," Benjamin yelled, slamming his hands down on the dining room table. "But now the goddamn British are making it even more difficult to immigrate there!"

"Oh yes, move to Palestine like your sister Rebekah. How I dreamt ever since I was a little girl to live on a *kibbutz* and become a farmer's wife," his mother retorted snidely, not sounding the least bit fazed by her husband's fury.

"Would that really be so bad?" Benjamin snapped back. "It's not as if you're getting to lead the life you once had, before this living nightmare started!"

"Oh, Benjamin, stop being so dramatic. People have always hated us Jews, but it's not the Middle Ages, we're not living in some *shtetl* in the Pale of Settlement, in fear of a pogrom. This is 1938. We live in Berlin, one of the world's most cosmopolitan and modern cities."

"You really don't get it, do you?" Benjamin said to Giselle, any previous sounds of anger and fury from his voice having been replaced by sadness and defeat. "This is just the beginning."

Sam inched quietly from the room and saw his father was pointing to the crumpled newspaper lying on the table. "What happened in Paris yesterday is just the beginning. I mean for God's sake, your children can no longer attend the schools they always have because now they're deemed 'Aryan' schools. The Nazis will use any excuse to further destroy us."

His father was referring to the assassination of a German diplomat in Paris the previous day at the hands of a teenage Jewish boy who had carried out the act in retribution for the expulsion of his family from Germany to Poland, where they were then trapped in limbo at the border between the two countries, neither country wanting them, and the Polish government loath to admit them and the thousands of other Polish Jews.

"Benjamin," his mother said, walking over to him and taking his hands within hers. "This all will pass; we'll get through it just like we did during the war. You'll see."

"Giselle," his father began, soberly pulling his hands from hers. "For as long as I've known you, I've always loved and admired your ability to see good when there's so much bad and hurt in the world. But now I fear your naiveté and ignoring what's going on around you is going to be the death of us all." Benjamin walked to the front door, put on his coat and hat, and quietly shut the door behind him.

Berlin, Germany
November 9, 1938

Since they were no longer allowed to go to school, their father had bade Sam and Marta work on their studies at home, telling them that he would not tolerate any "slacking" on their part. "I'm not sure why *Vati* even cares, it's not as if I'll be able to go to university next year," Sam grumbled to Marta as soon as their father was out of earshot while opening the pages of his calculus textbook although desperately wishing instead he could peruse the newest issue of *Architecture*.

When there came the sound of knocking on the front door, Sam and his sister looked at each other in surprise. They weren't expecting anyone and besides, their father had also expressly forbidden them to leave the apartment today. He didn't explicitly say why but Sam knew it had to do with the anti-Jewish sentiment that was splashed across all the German newspapers the previous day. Sam knew his father was most likely concerned that that same sentiment would be rife on the streets. And all because of the actions of a teenage boy his own age.

Whoever it was at the door hadn't been deterred by the fact that no one had answered it. The person just kept knocking.

"Oh, this is ridiculous," Marta said in a huff as she stood up to go answer it.

"Marta, don't," Sam said, trying to reach her, fearful of who was on the other side of the door, but he was too late. Marta swung open the door and there stood *Frau* von Hofmannsthal.

Usually the beacon of politeness and manners, today *Frau* von

Hofmannsthal was none of those things as she rushed in and said in a harried breath, "Quick, you must give me any valuables you have, anything you wouldn't want permanently taken from you. I will guard them and then in a few days return them."

"*Frau* von Hofmannsthal," Marta said, "What are you talking about?"

"Hildegard?" Sam, Marta, and *Frau* von Hofmannsthal all looked to see Giselle appear, a quizzical look on her face.

"Please," *Frau* von Hofmannsthal implored them. "There's no time to waste. All three of you, now, start collecting your valuables and we'll take them upstairs."

"Hildegard," Sam's mother said, the quizzical look on her face now replaced by one of annoyance. "I'm not going to give you anything until you tell me what's going on," crossing her arms over her chest.

"Giselle, we have been friends for nearly 20 years," *Frau* von Hofmannsthal. "You must know that I would never do anything to hurt you or your family. That I am only trying to look out for you. So please, please take my word and trust me on this."

Seeing the genuine look of care on *Frau* von Hofmannsthal's face, Sam's mother said, "*Kinder*, we will pay heed to *Frau* von Hofmannsthal's words."

And so for the next hour, Sam made repeated trips back and forth between his apartment and the apartment directly above theirs, taking away his family's most valuable possessions at the direction of his mother and Marta-a centuries' old gold-plated menorah, sterling silver candlesticks for *Shabbat*, a box containing his mother's jewelry (many of the pieces family heirlooms), his grandfather's pocket watch, and then two of his most prized possessions, banned by the Nazis since 1933-an English language edition of Ernest Hemingway's *A Farewell to Arms* and Erich Maria Remarque's *All Quiet on the*

Western Front. Sam knew these were not things the Nazis would want but knew he could get in serious trouble, and his family too, were they to be discovered.

On his first trip to the von Hofmannsthal apartment, Sam wondered what good it would do to put their prized possessions in the home of an ardent Nazi. And yet when she led him back to the "girls' room," the nursery that had been decorated for the little girls that she had never delivered alive, Sam understood. And then as if to confirm it, Hildegard told him quietly, "He has never once come in this room in all these years. He understands that it is my personal chapel for my dead baby girls." And then, almost as an afterthought added, "And he knows he is not welcome."

Before she bid them adieu, *Frau* von Hofmannsthal directed them, "do not answer the door and keep away from the non-curtained windows. And no matter what you hear, do not look out onto the streets."

She didn't say and they didn't ask, but Sam knew what she was advising, the safeguarding they had done to hide their valuables, that it all had to do with what 17 year old Herschel Grynszpan had done in Paris two days earlier.

When Sam's father returned home that night, he looked like he had aged 10 years. He had no reaction on his face when Giselle told him what had occurred earlier in the day with *Frau* von Hofmannsthal. He just sat there silently, not saying anything, appearing as if almost in a daze, looking like he had given up. That he wanted no more of this cruel , unimaginable life.

The mood in their apartment that night was tense and only grew more so when the sound of broken glass and fire trucks with their sirens wailing filtered up from the streets. Sam's mother ordered him and Marta to finally go to bed around midnight but severely said, "Stay away from the windows, no matter what!"

Sam knew he wouldn't be able to sleep that night, not with the sounds and noise from whatever was going on outside on the streets below. He closed his eyes periodically, trying to imagine what life was like in America, when there was loud pounding on the front door. Sam froze, immediately cognizant that it couldn't be *Frau* von Hofmannsthal this time. Sam hurriedly put on his robe and rushed out of his room to see Marta and his mother in a similar state of dress. Only his father was still fully dressed as he had been earlier in the day.

The pounding at the door continued, each whack causing his mother and Marta to wince as if they were the ones being beaten upon. And then there were loud, angry voices.

"Open this door immediately *Judenschwein* or we will break it down for you!"

And as if he was operated by a switch, Sam's father calmly went to the front door and unlocked it. The moment the latch was lifted Benjamin was set upon by three Brownshirts who pushed him to the ground, the biggest one then starting to kick him in the stomach and face.

"Stop, stop, *bitte*," his mother shrieked, on the verge of hysteria. Marta was sobbing uncontrollably, while Sam just stood there, frozen in horror at the scene taking place before him, wanting to do something, anything to help his father, but unable to move.

"Where are your valuables, Jewish bitch?" the skinny one demanded, turning to face his mother.

"Please stop hurting him and I will get them," Giselle implored.

Sam and Marta looked at each other, wondering what their mother could possibly give to these men considering all that they had hidden.

"Matthias, enough," the skinny one barked at the biggest one. He stopped beating Benjamin then but not before spitting on his father's limp body. It was the sight of tears streaming down his father's bloodied cheeks that alerted Sam his father was still alive and conscious. But it was this sight that broke Sam's heart. Knowing that this was what had finally broken his father.

"Get them!" the skinny one yelled at his mother who rushed off, followed by the big one. And then to Benjamin he said, "And you, get up and pack a bag. You're coming with us."

"But where are you taking him?" Marta asked, pulling on the man's sleeve. And then in stunned silence Sam watched as the skinny man backhanded his sister across the face, causing her to fall backwards to the ground.

Sam's father said nothing, just slowly and by the looks of it painfully, standing up and walking to his bedroom followed by the third Brownshirt who all this time had said and done nothing. Marta was quietly sobbing in the same spot where she had fallen.

"How old are you?" the skinny one said to Sam.

Sam said nothing, rooted in fear, too afraid to respond.

"A Jew and an idiot?" the skinny one cackled to the biggest one who had since returned to the entrance way with Giselle, her arms loaded down with goods. "I guess it's our lucky day," he chortled.

Anger finally starting to rise within him Sam answered, "Seventeen."

"What, Jew boy?" the skinny one asked.

"I'm 17," Sam said, louder this time.

"Leave him," the quiet Brownshirt said as he reemerged with Benjamin, who was carrying a small black suitcase. "We'll take the father for now. "We can always come back for him."

The big one then pushed Benjamin to start walking, barely allowing him the chance to put on his coat but not before Giselle and Marta rushed to him, throwing their arms around him until the skinny one roughly hauled them off, pushing them aside.

Sam said nothing to his father as he was led away, the tears finally starting to pool at the corners of his eyes. Before the door shut behind them, Sam's eyes locked with his father's, who mouthed the words, "I love you." Sam wondered if he would ever see his beloved *Vati* again.

After his father had been taken away, Sam's mother had collapsed on the floor like a puddle and stayed there, completely immobile. Sam and Marta had tried to get her to move, to get her to lie down in her bed but she wouldn't. So after a while they sat on the floor by the front door with her, each of them holding her hand within theirs.

Sam wasn't sure how much time had passed but knew it must have been morning from the faint light that was streaming in the front window. And then there came the sound of pounding at the door once more.

Knowing he needed to face whatever was going to happen now as stoically as his father had, for Sam wanted to remember his father as having been brave in the final moments he had spent with him, not broken, he walked to the door and opened it to find three new Brownshirts standing there. One of them was Max.

"Samuel Weiss?" the oldest looking one asked.

"Yes," Sam calmly replied.

"You're coming with us," he said, reaching out to take Sam's arm.

"May I pack a bag please?" he asked, his tone still calm and steady.

"You won't need one," the oldest one answered.

And then the one who appeared to be around Sam's and Max's age added mockingly, "For now," to which they both laughed. Max still said nothing, just displaying a steely glint in his hardened blue eyes, acting as if he hadn't been in this apartment a thousand times before, pretending that he didn't know the *Judenschwein* he was being tasked with removing.

Sam took a deep breath and allowed himself to be led out the door but not having the strength to look back at his mother and Marta, who still remained huddled on the floor together, not knowing if he would ever see either of them again.

Sam was loaded onto the back of a truck and when he climbed up, he saw other men already seated there, some around his age, others appearing older. But they all looked as wearied and frightened as he felt.

He hadn't been told where they were going so as the truck started to move, winding its way through the city's streets, he peered out a slit in one of the flaps. What he saw that morning he would never forget. There was broken glass and masonry everywhere, on the sidewalks, in the streets, the air thick with smoke, many of the city's buildings and *shuls* still on fire.

"I heard," a boy sitting on Sam's right whispered, "that the firemen weren't allowed to put any of the fires out. Only if there was going to be damage to a German business or home."

Sam didn't answer, choosing to ignore the young man and just continuing to look out, and also mentally trying to keep the nausea that was rising in his stomach at bay.

He could tell the truck was headed west towards Charlottenburg and when it approached the Kurfürstendamm, one of the city's most fashionable districts, he was stunned to see it in ruins.

Sam had never fully believed the stories his father had once told him about the war. How the landscapes of France and Belgium had been so decimated beyond words that they almost looked like they belonged in the pages of an H.G. Wells novel. But then he saw the streets of Berlin that morning, of his city, and knew his father had been telling the truth. And knew that human beings were capable of doing such horrific things.

As the truck drove by Café Wien and Zigeunerkeller, a restaurant and Viennese-style coffee house owned by friends of his parents, Sam wondered how the building was still intact, considering that *Herr* Kutschera was one of Berlin's most prominent Jews due to the immense popularity of his dining and drinking venues. But then he remembered his father saying to his mother one day that *Herr* Kutschera had been forced to "Aryanize" his establishments, that they were no longer "his." Sam didn't understand how someone's business, his livelihood, could just be stolen right out from under him, and no one doing anything to stop it. You could give it a fancy name like Aryanization but at the end of the day it was still outright theft and Sam knew it. He had been thankful at the time that his father just worked in a bank. Granted, he held a very high up position within the bank, but it wasn't like he owned a restaurant or shop that could just be snatched away.

When the truck finally stopped, storm troopers appeared at the back of the truck, lifting up the flap and yelling *"raus raus"* in harsh tones at the men inside to get down.

After jumping down, Sam was startled, realizing where he was. The truck had stopped on *Bleibtreustraße 17*, where Yva's (or *Frau* Neuländer-Simon as his mother insisted he and Marta call her) photography studio had once been located. Yva had been one of *Mutti's* greatest friends ever since Giselle had arrived in Berlin as a young woman. Their close friendship had always surprised Sam considering the fact that he found his mother somewhat conservative and not open to change, whereas Yva was renowned for being unorthodox in her work. (Sam and Marta were never taken to any of her exhibitions after the one and only time they featured nothing but nude photographs of both men and women). Not to mention, she worked in photography AS the photographer and not just the silent model like women had always done.

Sam remembered his mother saying Yva had moved after getting married but he didn't remember where. He wondered if she and her husband had survived the night unscathed, or if her new studio had been attacked. She was a pretty big name in Berlin and Sam had no doubt she was on some Nazi list.

And then being broken from his reverie, one of the storm troopers snarled, "You there! Start cleaning up this glass! And you!" he said, pointing to Sam, "Start scrubbing the sidewalks!"

Forced to get on his hands and knees and wear a sign that read *Ich bin ein schmutziger Jude*, I am a dirty Jew, Sam scrubbed for hours sidewalks he hadn't trashed and swept up glass he hadn't broken. His hands became raw and bloodied while the assailants, the true perpetrators of the heinous acts of violence from the night before watched, all the while hurling a barrage of non-stop insults at Sam and the others. As if it were all just a game to them...

When he returned home later that night, he breathed an audible sigh of relief when he spotted his sister's darkened form sitting in a wingback chair she had pulled to the entryway, not just waiting for him to return, but actually praying that he would.

On the long and dark walk back to the apartment, he had tried to push from his mind the horrible and sickening thoughts of dread- what if his mother and sister had been taken while he was gone?

So when he saw her there, safe and alive, he rushed over to her and took her in his arms, neither sibling speaking. The fierceness of their embrace negated the need for words.

In the days and months following *Kristallnacht*, the date of November 9 forever being known as "the night of broken glass," it was as if Sam had lost both of his parents. Although the family had received a note from Benjamin shortly after he was taken that terrible night, saying he was in a camp called Dachau, near Munich, but that he was being treated well and had enough to eat, they had never heard from him again. Sam kept up hope that his father was still alive and would walk back through the door at any moment but Marta was more of a realist. She immediately saw through the trite bullshit of the hastily handwritten message on the back of the rough and dirtied paper and bluntly said, "He's never coming back."

Of course this was done out of earshot of their mother. Not that it would have mattered anyway. She had been in a catatonic state ever since Benjamin Weiss had been beaten in front of her in their home and then taken away. Most days she barely got out of bed, only taking a sip of water or a spoonful of broth at Marta's cajoling, to placate her clearly worried children. But she said or did nothing, other than the decision she had made without consulting her children to stop living.

Frau von Hofmannsthal stopped by occasionally, usually giving them some *Reichsmarks* since they no longer had any income, but it was difficult for the wife of a high-ranking Nazi party member to do so without others in their building knowing. The only other Jewish family in the building had left the month before *Kristallnacht*, having been lucky enough to obtain visas to America. People liked to talk, to curry favors with party officials, but especially the building's concierge who was a fervent supporter and downright idolizer of Hitler.

Before she could even say, Marta had asked *Frau* von Hofmannsthal if she could hold onto the valuable possessions they had given her that November afternoon, until they "needed them."

Frau von Hofmannsthal had immediately said, "of course *libeling,* in fact I was going to suggest the same thing," lightly grazing Marta's cheek with the tips of her fingers.

Sam wondered when they would ever need an antique menorah again but knew that he must be missing something. Although he was the older sibling, Marta had become increasingly more mature these past few years, more savvy. In fact, ever since their father had been taken, it was as if she had become the parent of the house. Sam trusted Marta. In fact, she was the only person left that he would ever trust again.

 CHAPTER 23

Berlin, Germany
October 1939

"Oh Sam." Marta's tear streaked face was the first thing Sam saw upon entering their apartment.

"What? What is it? Is it *Vati*? Did you hear something?" Sam asked anxiously.

"It's *Mutti*. She's..." Marta's voice trailed off, quavering. "She's dead, Sam."

"What do you mean dead?" Sam asked incredulously. "She was alive this morning, I saw her," he said as he hurried to his parents' bedroom, hoping that his sister was just playing a cruel joke on him. But he stopped short upon entering the bedroom. His mother was lying on the bed in one of her elegant dresses, her hair and makeup done, clutching her wedding portrait between her hands. It looked to Sam as if she was just sleeping, a look of peacefulness and serenity radiating across her still beautiful features. But then he saw the pill bottles lying on the bedside table. He rushed over, frantically picking up the bottles and shaking them, only to discover what he already knew. They were empty.

"She never got over *Vati* being taken," Marta said quietly from

159

the doorframe. "She blamed herself. To her she had nothing else to live for."

"She had two goddamned children who still needed her," Sam cried out, punching the wall in a combination of both the immense shock and pain he was feeling. "Why weren't we enough to live for?" Sam asked, tears pouring down his cheeks now as he slid down the wall, suddenly feeling lightheaded.

Marta came over and sat next to him on the floor, taking his hand in hers, the lifeless and cold body of their once charming and vibrant mother mere inches from them.

"We have each other," she told him. "And starting now we live for each other."

The day their buried their mother was an unusually cold and dismally gray October day, even for Berlin. As they stood together on the damp ground at Weißensee Cemetery, Sam looked to his left and noticed off in the distance another burial taking place. Sam wondered about the circumstances of that person. Had they too killed themselves? Or just died of old age? Or had they willed themselves to die? Sam's mother had just expedited the process. He had no doubt whatsoever that given more time, his mother would have met the same fate.

"If he is indeed dead, then I wish *Vati* could be buried here too," Marta said as she looked down at the freshly shoveled dirt over their mother's final resting place. "I wish we could at least do that for her."

"She doesn't deserve a damn thing from us," Sam said, still unable to fully come to terms with what he was feeling over his mother's death. Was it just grief? Or anger that she could just abandon her children, leave them to face the horrors of war, the even more brutal persecution of their people.

"How can you say that, Sam?" Marta asked in a calm and placating manner.

"In fact," Sam began, "If there is indeed an afterlife, I hope her punishment for what she did is that she never sees *Vati* again," and with that he stormed off towards the entrance of the cemetery.

"I'm sorry about your *Mutti*."

A deep voice came from behind Sam, making him whirl around in surprise at the sight of Max standing there in his Waffen-SS uniform. Sam had come up from their apartment to their building's roof top, to escape Marta's emotional meddling, constantly asking him if he was all right, to escape the unrelenting memories he felt being there. And now here was Max, wearing a uniform that truly disgusted him, a wave of bile rising in his throat, the voices of the storm trooper monsters that horrible night in his apartment the year before and then the next day on the streets of Charlottenburg when he was publicly humiliated.

"What do you care?" Sam said bitterly, looking out onto the Berlin skyline. "To you she was just another Jew."

"She was still your *Mutti*," he answered. "And *Frau* Weiss was always a kind woman to me."

"Pity 'your people'," Sam said with a sneer, "didn't show that same kindness and respect the night you took my father and sent him and hundreds of others to their deaths," he shouted, whirling on Max.

With that, Max lunged at Sam, grabbing him by the collar, looking like he was going to punch Sam square in the face. Sam didn't flinch. In fact, the only look he displayed on his face at that moment was one of weary defeat, a look his father had worn so many times over the years, basically saying, "Go ahead, there's nothing more you can do or take from me."

Max abruptly let Sam go, fixing his hat so that the *Totenkopf,* the menacing skull that rested in the middle, was just so, and then brushing his hands off as if he had dirtied them. But Sam figured that Max probably thought he had, what by touching him and all, dirty Jew that he was.

"Watch yourself Weiss," Max said, a coldness in his tone Sam had never heard before. "Because if you're not careful, you'll wind up at *Prinz-Albrecht-Straße.* And now with both your parents...gone," (conveniently omitting mention of the fact that no one knew if Sam's father was indeed dead or not) "you wouldn't want to leave Marta all alone now, would you?" he added sweetly, as a stalking animal would say to its prey.

Prinz-Albrecht-Straße was the street that had become many a Berliner's worst nightmare for it was there that the *Reichssicherheitshauptamt,* the Reich Security Office, had made its headquarters, specifically where the Gestapo, the secret police, brought people it had arrested. A place where it was whispered that if you ever entered through its doors, you never left...at least not alive.

CHAPTER 24

Berlin, Germany
March 1941

"You should disappear."

The words coming from the wife of a high-ranking Nazi party official should have alarmed Sam, but it was *Frau* von Hofmannsthal they were talking about. Regardless of her fanatic husband and now son, Sam knew deep down, she didn't remotely condone what the Nazis were doing to the Jews. But as the wife of a high-ranking Nazi party official, she also felt powerless to stop it.

"But there's nowhere to go!" Marta said with a trace of both exasperation and sharpness in her tone, saying this to *Frau* von Hofmannsthal as if she were a child.

"No, I know it's too late to get out now, what with the world at war, the borders closed," *Frau* von Hofmannsthal said sadly, her eyes fixated on the sugar cube she was stirring round and round in her coffee cup, the sound of the silver spoon making a light clanging noise against the porcelain cup as if it were a motor. "I mean, disappear into the city."

"I don't understand," Sam said, the first thing he had uttered since they had arrived at *Frau* von Hofmannsthal's apartment, following the summons they had received in the form of a note which had been slipped under their door earlier in the day.

"Become someone else," she answered, finally looking up to meet Sam's eyes. "Neither of you look Aryan but you also don't look Jewish, which is good."

"We have no money, no family, how on earth would we survive?" Marta answered, always the pragmatist. "The apartment is all we have!"

"But this is our home," Sam said, still not fully understanding what the older woman was saying.

"I know people, I have friends," *Frau* von Hofmannsthal began tentatively, looking around as though someone could be listening, "who are willing to take in Jews, to help in keeping them safe." She paused then before continuing. "Your father was extremely well-known in Berlin, between his wealth and prestige from his position at the bank." Pursing her lips she added, "The Nazis knew of him. Why do you think he was one of the ones taken on that horrible night when others weren't?"

Neither Sam nor Marta spoke, the enormity but also the truth of what *Frau* von Hofmannsthal was saying slowly starting to sink in.

"You as his children are his sole surviving heirs," *Frau* von Hofmannsthal started, "and as such, will **not** go unnoticed by the Nazis."

"But how would our father ever find us if we're not here?" Sam asked.

It wasn't just Marta this time who gave Sam such a pitying look. Now *Frau* von Hofmannsthal did too. That she, like Marta, thought that their father was never coming back. And only Sam was a fool to harbor such naïve and childish hope that he was.

"But they've left us alone, *Frau* von Hofmannsthal," Marta said, "ever since the pogrom two years ago."

And they basically had. In the time since that horrible fateful night, there hadn't been any more middle of the night visits from storm troopers. Like all other Berlin Jews who were now impoverished after they were no longer allowed to practice a profession or enter the city's labor office, Marta and Sam had been assigned by the *Zentrale Dienststelle für Juden*, the Central Service Office for Jews, after registering there. Any ambitions Sam and Marta had once entertained of studying at university had been replaced by the forced labor they were assigned, both of them working 12 hour days at an armaments factory, Marta during the day, Sam at night. The work was physically grueling and often mentally unbearable, the pay pitiful, but Sam and Marta were just glad that they were still together.

Looking him squarely in the eye the older woman said, "I think it's going to get much, much worse before it gets better. I think what happened during the November pogrom is only the beginning. I don't think the Nazis are remotely done with their violence against the Jews."

Sam's head was spinning. How could anything possibly be worse than what had already happened to them? Everything that had been taken from them-their parents, their right to an education, money to live on.

"You will need to split up," *Frau* von Hofmannsthal said. "Right now you are Samuel and Marta Weiss, brother and sister. It will be safer if you separate, take on completely new identities where no one could possibly identify you from this life," she added waving her hand to indicate their apartment below.

"Absolutely not, "Sam said with an air of defiance. "Marta is all I have left now. I'm not going to risk losing her too."

"She's right," Marta said, putting her hand on top of Sam's in an attempt to mollify him. "I'd rather risk being apart now if it means we stay safe and we'll be together again after the war."

It was then that Sam noticed tears had started to stream down his sister's cheeks, the first time she had cried in over two years, for in all this time, it was his younger sister who had been the rock for him. "We need to do this for *Vati*, Sam," Marta said, tears still pooling at her eyes, but her voice as strong and determined as ever. "We both need to survive."

"So we can both become camel farmers," Sam joked, wanting more than anything to stop his sister's tears.

"To living on a *kibbutz* in Palestine one day," Marta said, raising her cup of coffee in a mock toast.

"*L'chaim,*" Sam answered, wanting more than anything for there always to be a reason to have life.

Max knew his mother had helped Sam and Marta disappear. He didn't think they had left Germany, in fact he was pretty confident they were still somewhere in Berlin, as to where he wasn't sure. He just knew that the apartment that had once been occupied on *Kronenstraße* by the family Weiss was now occupied by an SS Officer and his surly wife and their three ill-behaved children, along with two German shepherds who never seemed to stop barking.

Following his 17th birthday, Max had joined the Waffen-SS, the military branch of the *Schutzstaffel*, or as it was more commonly known, the SS, which was fast becoming the most powerful and feared organization in Germany. He had wanted to join when he turned 16, as he technically could have, and gone to work in one of the camps but his mother forbade it and in a rare display of parental solidarity, his father had agreed with her.

It was his father who had encouraged him to join the Waffen-SS and not just the main branch of the organization, which had been

Max's original plan. He thought this had to do with the fact that in the last war his father had been kept from fighting due to a heart murmur, a condition which stemmed from a bout of typhoid during his childhood. Max figured he would put any grandiose military aspirations he had once harbored in his son. And while Max would never have said this to anyone let alone his father, he also knew that his father had always been intensely jealous of *Herr* Weiss' prestigious military record during the last war, even receiving the Iron Cross for bravery displayed on the battlefield.

Max's father's aspirations for his son didn't just stop there. He had convinced Max it would be in his best interest to attend the *Führerschule des Sicherheitsdienstes,* the Führer School, in nearby Charlottenburg, for the purpose of obtaining a leadership role in the war. Max had initially balked at this, not wanting to be kept from the fighting, especially after the invasion of Poland in which Germany had enjoyed such a tremendous and decisive victory. He was so anxious to get to the front, not wanting to miss the fighting, but his father had assured him there would be more victories for Germany and that he would be part of them but not just as a lowly private, a *Schüze.* That he would soon be commanding men himself with the rank of *Untersturmführer,* a second lieutenant.

Max had heard talk of plans being made for a mass offensive in the east, for Germany to invade the Soviet Union and bring Stalin and his Communists to their feet, fixing that problem like the Nazis were fixing the Jews. No matter what, he wanted to be part of it when it happened. No, he planned on it.

❧ CHAPTER 25 ❧

Berlin, Germany
October 1941

Sam was tired, so very tired of it all. For months now he had lived in a series of grubby dark rooms, all of which had been foul-smelling and airless in the summer months and now with winter approaching, cold and dank. He was also so incredibly lonely, this life of a semi-nomad. But he supposed it was better than talk he had heard about Jews being crammed into apartments, sometimes with as many as 20 to a room in the city's poorest areas where they had been forced to go. He had even heard whispers that this was done to make it easy for the Nazis to 'round them up' once deportations to camps in the east began. Whether or not it was true Sam didn't know because the only thing that Berlin wasn't lacking in at the moment was rumors.

Although *Frau* von Hofmannsthal had obtained false identification cards for him and Marta, he was dreading the day he would have to show it, afraid that someone would immediately spot that it was fake or worse, wonder why a young man of 20 wasn't off at the front fighting. In patriotic Germany, dereliction of military duty was almost as bad as being a Jew, Sam had once jokingly thought to himself. As such he was also too afraid to regularly use the ration cards, the ones that matched his name with the name appearing on his fake identification card, Kurt Becker, and had him residing at an address he had never once been to. If he was caught with fake identification and ration cards, he knew that paired with being a Jew, death was almost surely an immediate, guaranteed fate. He had taken to wearing thick-rimmed glasses. Although his identity card didn't list him as being exempt from military service due to a medical condition, he knew that at least at first glance the glasses would cast off some initial doubt from passersby.

Sam discovered that the husband at one of the houses he had stayed at early on in his nomadic days was a black marketer, his business comprising the movement of goods, some stolen, the majority though sold in haste by individuals in desperate need of money. It was how Sam had procured a chocolate bar and an orange. But long after the sweet and succulent taste of that juicy orange and French chocolate had diminished from the recesses of his memory and the pit of his constantly hungry stomach, Sam knew he would need to be much more prudent with his limited money in the future if he was to survive.

Not that these days there was much of any food to really enjoy, not since the invasion of the Soviet Union had started four months ago. He had also heard that it was not going well, even if the German papers claimed differently, that it was just a matter of time before the German people enjoyed a momentous victory just as they had in Poland in '39. If he was staying someplace for more than a night, Sam gave what little money he had to his hosts, who would then treat him to a meal of often rotten potatoes, watery soup consisting of cabbage and beets, and coarse black bread.

Since they had split up, Sam and Marta met once a month, always on the third Monday, at a diner in Pankow. It was far enough away from their old home and life they thought it safe to be seen together there. It was only here that Sam felt safe enough to give in one of his 5-gram or 10-gram fat coupons that entitled him to a soup which was nothing more than salted water, a main dish consisting of meat topped with a gravy substitute, and two potatoes. He still always declined the dessert, not able to bring himself to consume the combination of water and artificial sweetener.

The first time he and Marta had dined there, they had both just looked at each other, trying not to laugh, when the waitress had set down their plates. Now however, with the food shortages that were prevalent everywhere and Sam's extreme reluctance to use ration cards for food, no longer did he take for granted the slop his mother would have deemed not fit for pigs, and instead rapidly and, he hated to admit it, greedily consumed it, the dessert notwithstanding.

That third Monday of the month, Sam made the long journey by U-Bahn and then tram to Vogel's Diner and was surprised upon arriving to discover that Marta was not already there, waiting for him as she always had. Neither sibling asked the other about their new life-where they were living, with whom they were living-nor did they speak of the past. They greeted each other as though they were friends who once a month simply met each other to catch up and speak of whimsical plans for the future, Sam wanting to go to America, Marta to Palestine.

Sam waited at the diner for nearly an hour but Marta never came. Every time the door opened, he would look up from his cup of hot water with licorice root that was steeping in it (what qualified as tea these days) hoping to see his sister's face only to be incredibly disappointed when it wasn't. Wanting to stay, for the whole hour he was there he had been telling himself in his head that there must be a perfectly logical explanation as to why she hadn't come-she had fallen ill, she had missed the tram, there was track work being done on the U-Bahn which was causing delays in service-he finally got up, knowing if he stayed any longer he would look suspicious, and left feeling incredibly dejected and forlorn over missing his sister.

He spent the next few days wondering what had happened to Marta and just hoping she was okay. Sam even considered returning to *Kronenstraße* and waiting outside for *Frau* von Hofmannsthal and asking her if she knew or had heard anything. But before he could even contemplate carrying out such a risky gambit, a small piece of paper was slipped under his door. Walking over, he bent down to retrieve it and read the words-

Meet me tomorrow under the Quadriga at 15:00.
H.v.H

It took Sam a moment to realize that the initials H.V.H. stood for Hildegard von Hofmannsthal for he was so used to referring to her as *Frau* von Hofmannsthal. Maybe she did have news about Marta, he thought. Maybe it's to tell him she had a found a way of smuggling his sister out of Germany. How he so hoped that was the case, that his beloved sister was finally safe.

"It's not safe here, let's walk into the park," *Frau* von Hofmannsthal said upon approaching Sam at the base of the Brandenburg Gate, the majestic neoclassical monument that had kept watch over the capital city for more than a century and a half now. Putting her arm through his, Sam and *Frau* von Hofmannsthal walked towards Tiergarten, appearing as though they were a mother and son out for a stroll before the sun went down and the temperatures dropped with the night air.

Once they were out of earshot from anyone who could possibly hear them, Sam asked frantically, "Is it about Lisbeth?" using Marta's middle name to refer to his sister.

Not once slowing down or even faltering in step, all the while looking straight ahead at the path she said, "There's no easy way to tell you this but she's gone, Sam. She was arrested earlier in the month and last Saturday, she was deported from Grunewald Station along with 1000 other Jews."

"Deported to where?" Sam asked in a hushed, strangled tone, all of a sudden feeling incredibly lightheaded.

"My sources say to Litzmannstadt. It's in Poland although it's called Lodz in Polish."

"Poland? Marta was German, why was she being sent to Poland? Why were any German Jews being sent there?" Sam wanted to cry out. Forcing himself to keep calm, he asked, "Why there?"

"There's a ghetto there apparently, for Jews. But the Jews were told they were being evacuated for work deployment in the East."

They kept walking until they came across a bench at which point *Frau* von Hofmannsthal sat, discreetly pulling Sam down beside her.

"So she was just arrested and deported?" Sam asked.

"No, she had been held for days at the *Levetzowstraße* Synagogue prior to the 18th," *Frau* von Hofmannsthal said tight-lipped, looking off into the distance of the dusk-filled park. "On the 18th they were forced to walk from *Levetzowstraße* to *Bahnhof* Grunewald where they then boarded the trains."

Sam desperately tried to think back to last Saturday and his voice broke, echoing the shattered feeling he felt inside himself when he said, "It rained all last Saturday." His poor, poor sister, who had done nothing wrong, who like him had lost everything, being forced to walk seven kilometers in the rain all alone, to what, a train that was possibly taking her to her death?

"How?"

Sam uttered the one word that he wanted an answer for.

"I was told that someone recognized her, that she wasn't the person she was claiming to be in her papers. And as such, the Gestapo arrested her."

Sam's heart felt it was breaking into a million pieces at that. His entire family was now truly taken from him. Would he ever see his sister again? Or would she become like his father, gone forever, never to return, just...like...that.

"Why are you doing any of this, why help us?" Sam asked.

Neither of them commented on the fact that there was no longer an "us," but rather just "me."

"Because a long time ago your father came to me and asked me to watch out for his family, to do everything I could to keep them safe if he wasn't able to be there."

As if he knew what was going to happen to him, Sam thought forlornly.

"I'm just one woman in an extremely precarious position," *Frau* von Hofmannsthal began. "And I'm no good to anyone if I get arrested. I do what I can to help as many as I can in my own way, but you and Marta, you mean everything to me," and then in a hushed whisper added, "now even more than my own Maximilian."

Standing up, she started smoothing out her gloves and quietly said to him, "Stay safe, my dear. There is talk of wanting to make all of Germany '*judenfrei*,' and so there will be more arrests, more deportations coming. I'll let you know if I hear anything," and with that she was gone, her petite figure and the dark coat she was wearing swallowed up by the approaching night sky.

Stay safe, Sam thought bitterly, watching the figure of his former best friend's mother grow smaller and smaller in the distance. As if that were remotely possible in a country that now wanted to make its borders 'free of Jews.'

❧ CHAPTER 26 ❧

Berlin, Germany
June 1942

When Sam would pass a Jew wearing the yellow badge, the Star of David, which immediately labeled who they were for everyone to see, he felt shame. Shame over seeing the sheer indignity that had befallen his people but also shame at himself. That he was trying to hide who he was and for what? His entire family had been taken from him, as if he had just snapped his fingers and poof, they were gone.

Jews had been required to wear the yellow badge for months now, ever since the previous September, but it was still jarring to him each and every time he saw one. Not to mention, he lived in constant fear that he would be outed by someone from his past, someone who wouldn't think twice about going to the Gestapo and reporting him if it meant the lives of themselves or their family could be kept safe. Sam knew that if that were to happen, he'd meet the same fate that had befallen his father and sister-whisked away, never to be seen or heard from again, most surely dead. He knew that now. He just didn't know why he couldn't have seen it sooner.

When word had gotten out that the invasion of the Soviet Union wasn't going well, that it had not turned into the quick, sure-fire victory that Hitler and his generals had envisioned it (like the campaign in Poland had been), life in Berlin had gotten even bleaker for its residents, but especially for Jews. In January of that year they were required to surrender all of their winter coats, warm clothing, and blankets, which were then sent to the German troops at the Eastern Front. As if they wouldn't need them themselves to make it through a harsh German winter, especially when wood was scarce. But maybe that was all part of the plan, to rid Germany of its Jewish problem. It didn't matter if they froze to death or were deported to their deaths. Just as long as they were gone from the Fatherland.

As the war raged on so did the problem of housing. Sam had spent the last of the money he had months ago, subletting a room in an apartment for 600 marks a month. At the time he had been pleased with the arrangement, happy to have somewhere to live for two months, free of having to worry over finding new accommodations, not to mention, the woman hadn't asked for his police registration, something he of course did not possess. But when another tenant in the building casually (or perhaps on purpose, Sam thought, a way of getting back at the woman by stirring the pot?) mentioned to him one day that the woman was only paying 150 marks a month for the entire apartment, he had felt sick. Sam was doing everything he could to just stay alive, to make it through another day as a Jew in Berlin and here was a woman purposely making a tidy profit at his expense. And all because she could. And they both knew it.

When the woman informed him that the rent was going up, on account of her growing "expenses," Sam had done the one thing he knew he could never do if he was to survive, if he was to go unnoticed. He showed emotion. He showed his utter vulnerability.

She said nothing following Sam's outburst and his plea for her to do the right thing by letting him stay, letting him pay her what he could considering how much he had already given her. But still she didn't speak, didn't say anything except stare, her green eyes taking on a measured, calculating glint.

She started walking towards the door but not before adding over her shoulder in an almost maniacal way, a sinister smile spreading across her face, "My brother works for the *Gestapo*." And with that she was gone. And so was Sam within the hour.

It had taken everything in Sam's power to not run as fast as he could from the apartment, frightened that as soon as the woman left the room she had called over to the Gestapo Headquarters on *Prinz-Albrecht-Straße*. But he knew if he started running, that would immediately attract attention and he'd almost certainly end up at *Prinz-Albrecht-Straße* anyway. A man who is guilty of nothing never runs, his father had once told him. So he had walked as calmly as he could to the U-Bahn station, aimlessly riding the underground for the next couple of hours, changing trains every couple of stations, all so he could disappear once more.

"Sam? Sam Weiss? Is that really you?"

Sam immediately froze at the mention of his name being spoken, unable to move, to do anything. He didn't recognize the voice from behind but was also too afraid to turn around and see who it was. Whether he would acknowledge the person or not, he knew he couldn't pretend to not have heard, as that would undoubtedly just attract more attention. So taking a deep inward breath he slowly turned and saw that it was Otto Fassbender, a former classmate of his from the *Berlinisches Gymnasium* and more importantly, a fellow Jew.

A fellow Jew who was also not wearing the yellow badge. And stereotypes be damned, looked entirely Jewish with his curly black hair, as if he'd just arrived from the *shtetl*. And most worrisome, was the last person Sam wanted to be seen with on the streets.

"What are you doing here, Otto?" Sam asked, not knowing what else to say, all the while trying to discreetly look around the streets of Wedding to see if there were any Nazis or SS lurking. He breathed a sigh of relief when he saw none, not to say there weren't any Gestapo in plainclothes ready to swoop in at any moment and arrest both of them.

Sam spent his days as a U-boat, which meant that during the day he would cruise "above water" by walking the streets of Berlin, always in neighborhoods where he couldn't be recognized by anyone from his old life but also removed enough from the homes he hid in at night, lest anyone make the connection. But he had to leave wherever he was hiding each morning before people were out on the streets leaving for work and school and then 12 hours later, sometimes more, in the cover of darkness, return home. The only way out of this was being permanently hidden but Sam had yet to encounter any German who was willing to take such an extreme risk by harboring a Jew indefinitely.

Since leaving the woman's apartment nearly a month ago, Sam moved houses every couple of days, no one wiling to hide a Jew for any longer lest their neighbors become suspicious of their new "houseguest," their recently arrived "relative" from another city. Everything from Sam's life had been whittled down into a shopping bag. Nothing more. Holding it made it look as if Sam had just been doing some shopping. It was thanks to *Frau* von Hofmannsthal and her underground network that was allowing him to survive, to still after all this time escape the clutches of the Nazis and avoid being arrested.

Ignoring Sam's question, Otto instead asked, "Say, you want to go somewhere and get a beer?"

That was absolutely the last thing Sam wanted to do. He needed to come up with an excuse fast, anything to get away from Otto. He continued down *Müllerstraße,* Otto walking alongside him uninvited, the traffic at a dead standstill. As they approached the entrance to the Leopoldplatz U-Bahn station, Sam did the only thing he could think of.

"Hey Otto, your laces are undone."

As Otto glanced down at his shoes, Sam hurried away making his break, racing down the steps of the station, appearing as if he was trying to catch an incoming train, instantly being swallowed up by the rush and throngs of other passengers around him.

There was something about his chance meeting with Otto that had left a deep pit in Sam's stomach. Hours later he sat alone in his tiny darkened room. The elderly widow he was staying with didn't allow him to have his own candle, lest any of her neighbors think there was someone else there but Sam didn't mind. She hadn't said anything to him that he would need to find someplace else to stay, so he could put up with the darkness for as long as he needed. He was totally exhausted, his head always in a heavy daze except when he was walking the streets always needing to be sharp and alert. He couldn't help but feel that it hadn't been a coincidence, running into Otto in Wedding on *Müllerstraße* of all streets. Otto without the yellow badge. Otto in perfect looking shoes, almost as if they were…new?

Sam reached down then and picked up his own shoes, running his fingers over the now worn and deteriorating leather soles. He knew there would come a point very soon where no amount of buffing and grease paint could make his shoes look anything but falling apart. But Otto appeared fresh and perfect, like there was no war going on, like they as Jews weren't being hunted and rounded up, like Otto didn't have a care in the world. Like he was immune to what was going on around him.

It was almost as if Otto had been looking for...him.

❧ CHAPTER 27 ❧

Berlin, Germany
February 1943

"Have you heard from Max lately?"

Frau von Hofmannsthal looked over at Sam in surprise. With her gaze directly upon him, it was only then that he noticed how much she had aged. During the times they had surreptitiously met over the last couple of years, Sam had never once asked about his former friend nor had *Frau* von Hofmannsthal ever brought him up. He knew the burden of guilt she must have carried, what with having a son in the Waffen-SS and then a husband who was personally involved in the deportation of thousands of Jews to camps and ghettos in the East from the high position he held with the national railway company. And how she thought that the work she was doing to help the Jews, Jews like Sam, would never be enough, would never remotely atone for the lives already taken by the likes of her son and husband.

"No, not recently," she replied, her tone somewhat veiled, he thought, as they continued walking through the Tiergarten, a young man with poor eyesight, taking his mother on a walk before dinner, not that there was much of dinner nowadays.

"Had he been in Stalingrad?" Sam couldn't help but asking. He was interested to hear where his once friend was fighting, if he had been one of the tens of thousands of German troops that had surrendered to Stalin's Red Army back in January who were now POWs there, in the Soviet Union of all places, a country that the Nazis despised. Although German media, that is state-censored media, had downplayed the defeat of the mighty Wehrmacht, when after 515 days, the Red Army had broken the German siege of Leningrad and Field Marshal von Paulus surrendered himself and 90,000 German troops less than two weeks later, Sam knew that things weren't looking good for Hitler at all. This, paired with Germany's defeat at El Alamein, provided a glimmer of hope that he was going to survive, that Germany would be defeated in the end after all. That the deaths of his parents and sister weren't in vain if he, Samuel Weiss, survived and could say the *Kaddish* for them.

"No, no," she said quietly, looking straight ahead. He was never that far east. I know he was in the Soviet Union, I think in the Baltics or Poland. He doesn't write to me, you know," she said, her voice slightly catching. "What I know is only what his father tells me."

Was that done on purpose, Sam wondered? Did Max suspect his mother's activities? Was not writing to her his way of punishing her?

"Are you okay *Frau* von Hofmannsthal?" Sam asked, feeling like this woman who had been so stoic and brave all these years was now finally cracking, or worse, resigning herself to mental defeat.

"And when this is all over? What then?" she asked, her eyes as blank and lifeless as the still dead winter landscape of the park.

Sam said nothing, unsure of what scenario *Frau* von Hofmannsthal was referring to-one in which Nazi Germany won the war? Or one in which it was defeated? Both scenarios still meant that Sam's life would never be the same again, the losses insurmountable.

Berlin, Germany
November 1943

The first time Sam had heard the air-raid siren go off he had been too afraid to go to the bomb shelter. He was fearful that SS and Gestapo officers used air raids as hunting season, a prime chance to roundup Jews in hiding, anyone with false papers, when everyone was trapped deep inside with nowhere to go. He reasoned that it was better to take his chances and be instantly killed by a falling bomb then be arrested and sent east to an unknown fate that awaited him, which he thought seemed a lot worse.

Even on the nights of November 18 and 19 when the sky was alight with hundreds of British bomber planes, the ground seeming to reverberate with each bomb that was dropped, Sam wasn't scared. He just looked up at the sky in wondrous amazement, wishing he was up there himself in one of those planes, helping in the fight against evil, the fight against his homeland.

"By surviving, you are fighting."

Sam whirled around to see his tiny, elderly landlady standing behind him, her eyes on him.

"I thought you had gone to the shelter," Sam said, moving to stand in the corners of darkness once more, not in the open space of the yard as he had been doing, hoping she wasn't mad at him for having come outside.

"I never go, I always stay in my room. But when I heard you creeping outside, I decided to see these planes myself."

"I'm sorry *Frau*, I did-"

She cut him off then with a wave of her hand. "Don't worry. I think we are the only Berliners stupid enough to not go to the shelters. I know why you don't, and you know why I don't?" she asked him, to which he shook his head no.

"I'm 74 years old. I've lived through two wars before this one and buried two husbands and three sons, two of whom died in the last war. I'm ready to go and join them at any time. God will tell me when it's my time to go but when I do, I want to go from here," she said, bobbing her head at her house. "Not in some shelter amongst strangers, most of whom would denounce you if it meant getting some sugar or coffee."

Sam looked at her, amazed. In the year now that he had been staying with the widow, she had barely said more than a few words to him. She wasn't mean to him but neither was she kind. Sam had never once thought she hated him, hated Jews, she just more hated what Hitler and the Nazis had done to her country, their country, and by giving this Jew boy shelter when no one else would, she was carrying out her very own act of resistance against the Third Reich, even if it meant the cost of her own life were she ever caught.

It was almost as if by talking about it, the elderly widow had made her desire to die at home amongst the memories of her dead relatives that surrounded her in their brass plated picture frames come true for less than a week later, British planes dropped a bevy of bombs on the heart of the city, causing widespread damage but also taking the life of the woman who had selflessly risked her life for him for months but whose name Sam didn't even know. She had always just been "the widow" to him; it's how she had wanted it.

The moment Sam had seen the bomb drop and knew it was going to hit the house, he had for a brief moment contemplated not moving but rather staying exactly where he was, rooted in place in the small patch of yard of the widow's house, ready to come home to his parents and sister again, wherever that was. But then he remembered the widow's words to him a few nights earlier, that by surviving, he was fighting. And so with her words echoing strongly in his head, he ran as fast as he could away from the house but not before the bomb struck, the impact making Sam almost fly in the air, like he had thought the Negro Olympian Jesse Owens had looked all those years earlier when he had watched him compete in the games at the *Olympiastadion* winning medal after medal. And then he blacked out.

When Sam came to, he didn't know how much time had passed since he had lost consciousness. He woke to find what had previously been a street now nothing but a landscape of rubble and half-standing buildings, many of which were on fire, the massive flames blowing erratically against the dark night sky, the air so thick and heavy with smoke and soot that he could almost taste it. When he looked back at what had been the widow's house he just hoped that she had gone quickly, that she hadn't suffered.

He stood up then, thankful for the cold temperatures which had made Sam get in the habit of sleeping in both his coat and worn shoes, the former of which contained his false identity card. He still was loath to use it but knew it was better to have it on him than have nothing at all to show if asked. The contents of his shopping bag were forever gone, and he had no way of replacing them. He was literally left with only the clothes on his back, he thought ruefully to himself. But at least he had his coat, for without it, Sam knew he could easily freeze to death, not to mention arouse unwanted suspicion for a person without a coat in winter only could mean one thing-that they were trying to evade arrest.

Sam was pretty sure the all clear hadn't been sounded yet but he knew he needed to get away from there, before daylight broke when the authorities and other people would come looking for survivors and anything they could possibly forage from the damage. And so he started walking, his head down, his hands tightly pressed in his threadbare coat pockets. He walked with no purpose or destination in mind that night, but because he truly had nowhere else to go; it was the only thing he could think to do.

As he walked the streets, each step he took seemed heavier than the last one, and he almost didn't recognize the city where he had spent his entire life. He remembered then his father talking of the decimated landscapes of the Western Front during the last war, beautiful towns and villages in France and Belgium completely destroyed from the effects of war, and yet this was Berlin. This wasn't a random village on the map, this was one of the world's most prominent cities and tonight it was nothing more than a smoldering ruin.

Sam had always been indifferent to religion, something his also indifferent parents had never had a problem with. He had dutifully attended services at the *Neue Synagoge* on the High Holy days each year because his father had told him when he was a small child that it was what "all good Jews did." As if that explained to an eight year old why twice a year he and his father wore *kippahs* on their heads and listened to singing and talking in a language that they didn't know inside the massive building that looked straight out of *1001 Arabian Nights*. When he saw however, the destroyed shell of the *Kaiser-Wilhelm-Gedächtniskirche*, the church named after the grandfather of Germany's last emperor, Sam couldn't help but wonder over the higher up powers that be. He knew from forbidden BBC broadcasts he had once listened to years ago that London's great St. Paul's Cathedral had survived night after night of brutal air attacks from the German *Luftwaffe* during the height of the *Blitzkrieg* even when everything else around it had been destroyed, and yet hundreds of miles away, a German church was obliterated, just like that. Was it a sign that even God himself was rooting for the Allies to win? For Hitler and his Nazis to be forever beaten?

And when he arrived at *Kroenstraße*, even though he knew he shouldn't be anywhere near his former home on the chance that someone would recognize him, and saw the building heavily damaged and on fire, he only hoped that *Frau* von Hofmannsthal was safe someplace else. He decided then and there seeing his former home ablaze, the home he had grown up in and held such wonderful memories of his parents and sister, that no, there was no God anymore. At least not in Nazi Germany.

CHAPTER 28

Berlin, Germany
December 1943

Ever since the November bombings, Sam had been constantly on the run, having to change hiding places almost every night it. With the losses in North Africa, the Americans joining in the fight on the side of the Allies, and of course, Germany's surrender to the Soviet Union, the German people were tired, frightened, and weary of anything that could potentially put them and their families in harm's way. Ever since Berlin had been declared *judenfrei* back in May the Gestapo and SS had become more ruthless in their quest to search out every last Jew in hiding and it wouldn't make *Herr* Hitler happy at all if Berlin was indeed not "free of Jews" as had been originally declared. The noose was bearing down upon each and every German that stood in opposition against the Nazis but no one felt the precariousness of it all more than a person like Sam, a Jew not permanently hidden.

He often wondered what it would have been like had he been in permanent hiding all this time, "tucked" away until it was safe to come out again, as if he were some fragile toy that only an older, well-behaved child could play with. He wondered would it have been better, easier even, if he had had this option. Would he have had the mental endurance to not breathe in fresh air for months, years even, to not walk the streets and relive memories in his mind that he had of his parents and sister? Could he have been capable of entering a small, perhaps even claustrophobic space and know he could never come out again until the war was over? Being a U-boat meant he was constantly hungry and tired, exhausted even, but he still had his freedom, he still had the ability, the sheer pleasure of going outside.

Sam wasn't sure if one was better than the other. He only knew that if it weren't for *Frau* von Hofmannsthal's extensive list of contacts from her work in the underground, he would have been arrested and deported a long time ago. He tried telling himself, this had to be better, right? By surviving you are fighting were the words he said over and over in his head each night when he tried to fall asleep, when he hoped and prayed that the air-siren warning wouldn't go off, that a bomb wouldn't drop on his head (his hiders always explicitly forbade him from leaving even against the threat of an air raid lest anyone see him) because the simple truth was he **did** want to survive, he truly wanted nothing more than to live.

Sam told himself he was most likely being paranoid but he couldn't shake the feeling that someone was following him. He had felt this way for days now; no matter where he was in the city, he had a strange sensation that someone was always there, watching him.

He knew that when he was outside, he needed to look natural to anyone who saw him, like he had every right to be walking the streets, like he still belonged on them. Exuding confidence was key to staying safe and undetected; he knew he needed to project this image every time he stepped outside. But it took every last ounce of restraint to not constantly be looking over his shoulder. Sam was cognizant of the fact that such an action would immediately make him look

THE DEAD ARE RESTING

suspicious, like he had something to hide. It wasn't just the SS or Gestapo he feared, but more the average German citizen who craved the praise of Hitler more than that of God and who fervently believed that by turning in a Jew, even if it was a fellow German, he was doing his part for the war effort, all for the glory and triumph of the Third Reich.

When he thought he'd spotted Otto Fassbender again one day in Charlottenburg across the street from where he had stopped to tie his worn and frayed laces, he closed his eyes, silently chiding himself that he was crazy, that there was no way Otto would be on the same street as him at the very same time. No, he hadn't seen him. After he had opened his eyes again, whoever had been there across the street was now gone, as if he had vanished into thin air. And just then from behind he heard someone say-

"*Herr* Weiss, you're under arrest," as Sam felt the barrel of a gun against the nape of his neck, the unmistakable sound of its cocking reverberating loudly on the quiet and desolate streets, Charlottenburg having been badly damaged during the prior month's aerial bombings, ruin and destruction still everywhere.

"I suggest you stand up and turn around slowly with your hands up. Try anything and I'll shoot," the man with the gun said. Were the situation not so dire, Sam would have laughed at the absurdity of what the man had just said, like they were acting out a scene from some Hollywood picture.

But he did as he was told and came face to face with his captor. For a fleeting moment he thought about lying, about telling this man his name wasn't Weiss, showing him his false identity card to prove it. But when the man held out his Gestapo card to him, any last remaining trace of confidence and bravery he had once had while walking the streets of Berlin vanished then and there. The game of survival was over and he had lost.

As he was being led to the waiting black Mercedes-Benz, there was Otto Fassbender standing against a building on the other side of Spandauer Damm.

"Good thing your laces were undone, eh Weiss?"

Sam could still hear the loud sound of Otto's laughter ringing out even as the car door was shut behind him.

He was taken to the *Große Hamburger Straße* detention center. He immediately recognized where he was because as a child his *Tante* Rebekah had once taken him and Marta there to show them the city's oldest and first Jewish cemetery, an outing his parents had happily passed on. But as Sam was being led from the car into the tall building with barred windows, he couldn't see a single grave. All he saw were the air raid shelters that now stood in their place. His people, who had been dead for more than 100 years, for he remembered *Tante* Rebekah saying the cemetery had reached capacity sometime in the early 19th century, were not left to rest for all of time. Sam wondered then if his *mutti's* grave had been desecrated too. If even one trace of the once vibrant and historically rich Jewish life that had existed in Berlin for centuries would be left when the war was finally over.

As Sam was the only remaining member of his family still alive, the men interrogating him had only been interested in him telling them the names of 10 Jews living illegally in the capital and where they could be found. He was told that if he did that, he could stay there till the end of the war and avoid being deported east to one of the camps.

Before he could stop himself, Sam laughed out loud at this, which resulted in him getting backhanded across the face. But it was ludicrous, the idea that he knew one Jew living illegally, let alone 10. Did they not understand that ever since he had separated from his sister nearly two years ago, he had been completely on his own, that he, Samuel Weiss, had ceased to exist until now? And any talking he had done all these months, outside of the conversations he had constantly carried on with himself in his head, had been minimal and always with non-Jews?

After getting roughed up a bit more, a trickle of blood running down the corners of his mouth, he spit out the name, "Otto Fassbender."

His interrogators became quiet then, their silence confirming to Sam what he had feared since the day Otto had spotted him in Wedding. Fassbender, he was none other than a "Jew catcher," a Jew who worked for the Gestapo, which made him even worse than they were.

The interrogations stopped after that.

The entire time Sam had been locked inside the *Große Hamburger Straße* detention center, he heard other Jews mention the name Auschwitz. They whispered that this Auschwitz was where they were being sent, a work camp in the East, presumably Poland. A country and culture of undesirables according to Nazi ideology, so naturally that's where they would send the German Jews.

Of course, nothing that was whispered in clipped, harsh tones in the perpetually dark and cold rooms at *Große Hamburger Straße* was actually known to be true. It was all just rumor, stories varying wildly from person to person, even amongst families. But the one consistent thread was that Auschwitz was a place you didn't want to be sent to.

As Sam stood with the other Jews on Platform 17 at Grunewald Station, a cold, steady rain beating down upon them, his now threadbare coat no longer a match for the harsh temperatures of a Berlin winter, he wondered to himself how much more could he endure, or more aptly, how much more was he willing to endure.

Since his arrest, days ago (or was it weeks?) Sam had lost track of what day it was, no longer able to spot the date on the front page of newspapers for sale when he used to roam the city. He had spoken very little, preferring to keep to himself. Unlike many of the other detainees at *Große Hamburger Straße*, Sam was all alone. And at this point in "the game," as he ruefully called it, he had no desire whatsoever to form any sort of attachment to another person. Caring about someone else caused nothing but pain and grief. So that's why he was surprised when he heard a voice from behind him speaking.

"Tonight is the first night of Hanukkah."

Sam turned around to see a man who looked to be his father's age talking to him. Before he could say anything the man continued on as if he were giving a lesson.

"Today is the 25th day of *Kislev*, a date when we remember the rededication of the Second Temple in Jerusalem, when our ancestors the Maccabees successfully rebelled against Antiochus IV Epiphanes."

Sam stared at the man in disbelief. He seemed not only oblivious to the cold and the rain but also to the children and babies who were crying, to the mothers trying to comfort them, and to the sounds of misery and suffering that were omnipresent.

Sam replied by asking the only thing he could think of, "How on earth do you know that?"

"I know it doesn't look it," the man said, jokingly indicating his appearance. "But I was a rabbi for many years, at a small synagogue in Potsdam. When I went underground, I shaved off my beard and *payot*."

"Your what?" Sam asked, never having heard this word, *payot*, before.

"Ahh, I take it you are not an observant Jew," the man said with a smile.

Sam didn't know what to say. The old him would have responded with a sarcastic retort, that no, he lived life like it was the 20th century in one of the world's greatest cities and not the 18th century in some *shtetl* in the Pale of Settlement. But the Sam of now, the one who had lost everything and everyone?

"No, I'm sorry, I'm not," he answered.

"I'm not here to judge, my boy," the man said kindly. "And nor is God, even though I myself, a highly religious man, find it hard to believe at times that He still exists, that He'd let so much evil and suffering prevail against our people. But I don't ever give up, even with everything that's been lost and taken from me all these years. I simply don't give up," he said and then added, "and neither should you."

Sam was about to say, at least deep down, he had already given up, that he was simply going through the motions of living anymore, accepting whatever fate awaited him in Poland. But instead he joked, "Well, since we're being deported today, on the first day of Hanukkah, maybe it's God's way of telling us we should rebel against the Nazis, that we're the modern-day Maccabees, and Hitler is Antiochus. The Maccabees were successful in their fight, why can't-"

But Sam's words were cut off by the loud blaring of a train whistle and then moments later, the appearance of a row of faded red freight cars slowly pulling into the station. He didn't need to ask to know that the freight cars were for them. When the people around him noticed the windowless cars that had now come to a stop before them, chaos ensued. Children and babies who had only been whimpering softly into the cloth of their mother's skirts and blouses just moments earlier were now wailing uncontrollably, this a result of the sound and actions of their panicked parents.

Sam looked back at the rabbi now and just like before, he still appeared oblivious to the scene before him. But then in a tone of almost disconcerting calm he said to Sam, "Our destination is to die. Why should we expect anything else?"

⚜ CHAPTER 29 ⚜

Auschwitz Camp
Oświęcim, Poland
June 1944

Judentransport aus den Deutschland-Berlin Bahnhof Grunewald
21. Dezember 1943
222. Weiss Samuel 29.6.21

Max stared down at the transport list in his shaking hands. He had done it, he had found Sam. But then he stopped, mentally reminding himself that the transport list was half a year old and that one of the many things he had learned in his brief time at Auschwitz thus far was that anything older than a day could be considered outdated, a thing of the past. Just because Sam had been sent here, sent to Auschwitz, didn't necessarily mean that he was still here six months later, that he hadn't been liquidated.

It had taken Max and *Schüze* Kohler, the lowly private who had been assigned to assist him when he arrived at the camp, weeks to simply find this transport list, the one Max knew to contain Sam's name. *Schüze* Kohler hadn't asked why he was being tasked with such a random request, he had simply clicked his heels together and called out almost triumphantly the Nazi salute, *Sieg Heil.* Kohler was barely 18 and seemed eager to please his superiors. He was a boy with an almost unhealthy lust for war, which is why Max wondered why Kohler had been assigned to the camp and wasn't off at the front. But then Max knew of men whose desire for the complete extermination of the Jews was what brought them here, to a place like Auschwitz, and not fighting the Allies in battle.

After being injured early on in the Battle of Kursk when he had been hit by grenade splinters in both his head and leg, his commander had told him he was no longer fit for front-line duty, which Max had expected. He had spent weeks in a field hospital before finally being transferred back home to Berlin, where he then spent months recovering at the Charité, the city's famous hospital.

Originally he had been assigned to Sachsenhausen, a camp not far from the capital. But then on one of his father's visits to see him, he had informed Max he had pulled some strings and gotten him an even better assignment, working at the *Reichssicherheitshauptamt*, the main security office of the Reich, the place whose very name people were afraid of. "You're a *Hauptsturmführer* now, you can't be working at a lowly camp that houses nothing but political prisoners and Communists," his father had told him when Max had balked at the idea of working at the headquarters on *Prinz-Albrecht-Straße.* "You must be at the center of it all!" he had eagerly told his less than excited son.

And so Max had returned home, sleeping in the same bed he had growing up, but also seeing images of Sam everywhere he looked. He never would tell his father this but that was the main reason why he hadn't wanted to remain in Berlin. The ghost of his once best friend was everywhere, taunting him endlessly.

There were also the nightmares that played out in his head over and over each night, of scenes he had witnessed in the Soviet Union shortly after arriving there. Images that didn't torment him as a soldier, but rather as a human being, ones that made him wake up in his childhood bed, drenched in sweat.

Initially Max had been excited over the prospect of his first ever assignment for the Fatherland, going to the godless Soviet Union and forever ridding it of "Judeo-Bolshevism" which had poisoned the land for far too long so that one day it might be pure enough to repopulate it with Germans. But then he witnessed an operation of the *Einsatzgruppen*, a special task force that was responsible for taking care of the Jewish Question in German-occupied countries. It had been in a small town in Ukraine in which all of the Jews were rounded up, forced to dig trenches, 40 meters long by five meters wide and three meters deep (a figure he would remember for the rest of his life, he knew), and then made to undress, this of course after handing over their valuables to the authorities. At first he had been unnerved, seeing the naked bodies of so many, young and old, fat and skinny, a few even beautiful even though they were Yids. And then the rest happened so fast. They were herded down into the ravine, made to lie down, and then shot in the back of the head or neck. And this went on for hours upon hours. A new group would then be led down into the ravine and forced to lie down in rows on top of the bodies of the earlier victims, where they were then shot.

He had been told that operations throughout the Soviet Union were all like that, although in some instances, small villages mainly where there were fewer inhabitants, the Jews were simply rounded up, locked inside buildings, and just burned alive, wiping both the village and the Jews that lived there from existence.

In the time he had been gone, Max's relationship with his mother had deteriorated to the point that there was none. She had never written him when he had been away fighting and had only been to visit him twice during the months he had spent recovering at the

Charité, something he felt was done more out of obligation and public opinion than anything else. Once he was back in his childhood home, his mother had treated Max with politeness but also a trace of coldness, as if he were no longer her son but rather a stranger taking up residence in her home. As if she knew what he had witnessed, as if he were somehow responsible.

His mother clearly couldn't stand being around him anymore while Max couldn't stand being around his father. One evening at dinner, his father had boasted proudly that the Reichsbahn was transporting hundreds of thousands of Jews on its trains throughout Nazi-occupied Europe to the camps and he was becoming "famously" rich as a result. "We were rich before the war but goddamn it," his father had said excitedly, slamming his hand down on the mahogany dining room table, "once it's all over we'll be even richer!" His mother had said nothing and his father hadn't seemed to care at his wife's lack of interest and participation in the conversation. Before the war, there had always been a sort of dysfunctional, almost spirited animosity between his parents. Now, Max's father seemed to ignore his mother altogether, although she didn't seem to mind. He would never ask but Max wondered if she missed Marta and *Frau* Weiss. At one point, the three had been inseparable.

It was a combination of the palpable tension at home and his feeling bored and uninspired with his desk job at the *Reichssicherheitshauptamt* that made Max go to his superior there and ask to be reassigned to one of the extermination camps in Poland, the country that was doing the best at carrying out the Final Solution. He had noted that he didn't care which camp it was, just one where his father couldn't step in as he had done in the past and inhibit Max from doing what he wanted to do the most, serving the *Führer* in the best way that he could. And the best way was not him sitting at a desk in a building on *Prinz-Albrecht-Straße* and behaving as if there hadn't been a war on the last four years between the nightly parties and the nonstop champagne and other luxury goods that for most people hadn't graced their plates since before the war.

A firm knock sounded on Max's door.

"Come in," he called out, annoyed.

The door opened up as *Schüze* Kohler entered.

"*Sieg Heil,*" the younger man said, giving the Nazi salute.

"*Sieg Heil,*" Max said, not looking up, his eyes fixated on the transport list that had Sam's name on it.

"You wanted to see me *Hauptsturmführer*?" Kohler said.

"Yes," Max began, wanting to sound casual and indifferent over what he was about to ask. "I need you to go to the records office and find out if this Samuel Weiss is still a prisoner here. We know he arrived here at Auschwitz last December from Berlin. I need to determine if he was gassed upon arrival or assigned to a work detail. That will be all *Schüze* Kohler," Max said dismissively, pretending to focus his eyes on the stack of papers in front of him, not wanting to give the younger man a moment to ask any questions as to the purpose of this further inquiry.

"*Ya, Hauptsturmführer,*" Kohler said, clicking his boots together as he proffered yet another loud and robust "*Sieg Heil,*" to which Max responded with an almost feeble "*Sieg Heil.*" When the door was shut firmly behind the younger man, Max breathed an audible sigh of relief and removed from his front pocket a folded black and white square photograph that showed two young boys around the age of 10, each arm draped over the other's, smiling broadly. And if you looked close enough at the photo, you'd swear they were brothers.

"He's here, *Hauptsturmführer,*" Kohler whispered into his ear.

"If you'll excuse me, gentlemen," Max said to his fellow officers who he was dining with that night, "an urgent matter has come up that I must see to." Standing up from his chair, he saluted them all with a "*Sieg Heil*," and left the room, Kohler hurrying behind, knowing to not say a thing until they were safely out of earshot of the other men.

Once they were outside, the sun starting its slow descent as it cast brilliant shades of red and orange across the sky, Max turned to Kohler and asked impatiently, "so?"

"Oh *ya Hauptsturmführer,*" Kohler hurriedly began as he rustled the papers he carried under his arm. "Prisoner number 126296. Here's his registration card," handing Max the card that all prisoners received after surrendering their clothes and other valuables once they arrived at the camp. But most importantly these cards contained the prisoner's camp number, which is how they were known; the names they had been known by their entire lives ceased to exist once they entered Auschwitz.

Flipping through the documents, Max read that Sam was in the men's camp, in sector BIId and that he worked in Kanada II. So even in a place like Auschwitz, Max sardonically thought to himself, Sam was still winning, getting a plush assignment like sorting the baggage and other valuables of the deportees.

"Speak to his *Blockführer* and have him brought to me at once," Max said to Kohler. "I need to hold onto this," referring to the folder which contained the records on Sam, "for the time being."

"*Ya, Hauptsturmführer,*" Kohler said, hurrying away, not even remembering to salute Max, so eager to please was he. But Max didn't care in the least. He was going to see Sam again.

✤ CHAPTER 30 ✤

Max nervously paced the small confines of his office as if he were waiting for a call from *der Führer* himself. When was the last time he had seen Sam, Max wondered to himself. *Kristallnacht?* No, he had seen Sam after Sam's *mutti* had died, or killed herself he thought more accurately. A Jew going effortlessly. If only they all could be like that, fondly remembering *Frau* Weiss then and her selfless action.

A strong knock sounded on his door.

"Come in," Max barked, his heart racing as he said those words.

The door opened and Max froze at what he saw. Before him stood what appeared to be an old man. He almost shuffled into the room, dragging his feet as he walked. The man's skin was an ashen color, his cheeks gaunt and sunken in. The once vibrant and thick chestnut curls were no more, replaced by a craggly brown stubble that covered the man's head. At closer examination, Max noticed a small but thick scar on the right side of his head, just above his ear.

"Sam?" Max asked incredulously.

Sam said nothing, still looking down at his feet.

"*Hauptsturmführer* von Hofmannsthal is talking to you," *Schüze* Kohler barked at Sam, hitting him on the back with his baton which made Sam wince in pain and slightly bend over.

"That will be enough, *Schüze* Kohler," Max said firmly. "You may go."

"*Sieg Heil*," Kohler said, saluting Max then shutting the door behind him.

"Sam?" Max said again, so desperately wanting to hear his voice. And then before he thought fully about what he was doing he said, "Please sit down. Can I get you anything?"

"I want nothing from you," Sam said in a quiet yet steely voice, still not looking up from the oversized clogs he wore.

So he is going to make this difficult Max thought, swearing softly under his breath. He briefly entertained the idea about ordering him to talk, threatening Sam with a beating administered by Kohler, who Max knew would be all-too-pleased to carry out this directive. But he thought better of it. Max had time and it wasn't as if Sam was going anywhere anytime soon.

The idea came to Max the very next day. He would have Sam transferred from the Kanada to work for him, to clean his office and living quarters and prepare his meals when he wanted to be alone and didn't want to dine in the officers' dining room. I mean, a prisoner couldn't get a more luxurious work assignment than that, he thought, immensely pleased with himself.

But Sam seemed indifferent to his new position. He did what was asked of him but nothing more, only answering in one or two word answers, purposely staying silent if Max asked anything of a more personal nature. The more Max pushed, became aggressive, the more defiant Sam seemed to become with his silence.

At first Max considered threatening Sam with the gas chambers but saw after a few days that wouldn't make a difference. Sam, he observed, didn't seem to care about living, about anything in life anymore. The once vibrant, inquisitive boy he had once known, had been best friends with, was no more. It was as if he was dead. And maybe that's what he wanted. But Max was damned if he was going to give this easy out to him. No, he had to think of something better.

"If you don't stop your sullen behavior and answer me when I address you," Max said evenly as Sam was loading the coffee service back onto the tray, "then I will transfer you to work in the *Sonderkommando*."

And at the brief pause in Sam's movement, Max saw he had found the one thing that could elicit a reaction from him. Sam perhaps wanted to die, didn't have any desire to still live, but he had no desire to work in the crematorium where the slave laborers processed and disposed of the bodies of those murdered in the gas chambers.

Smiling almost gleefully as if there was no greater pleasure than this moment where their respective roles were so carefully delineated, Max said, "So what will it be?"

And then for the first time in days, Sam spoke, not sounding as if he were reciting from a script. "What do you want to know?"

"Everything. Tell me everything since the last time I saw you, and most importantly, how you evaded deportation for so long when Berlin had been declared *judenfrei* in May of 1943 and you weren't sent here until December."

Auschwitz Camp
Oświęcim, Poland
July 1944

"Will you be joining us at Solahütte this weekend *Hauptsturmführer* von Hofmannsthal?"

Max looked up at the mention of his name and saw that *Oberführer* Richter was addressing him.

"Solahütte?" Max said, repeating the name as if it were a question. "I'm afraid I'm not familiar with it."

"Leave it to these idiots here," *Oberführer* Richter said, pointing to Georg, Oskar, and Johannes, three fellow SS officers, although Johannes held a higher rank than the other men, "to scrimp on orientation when Solahütte is perhaps the only redeemable thing about the filth that is this country." And then he took a big swig of his beer but rather than replacing it on the table in front of him, he continued to hold it mid-air as if he were going to offer a toast.

The men waited for him to continue, not wanting to interrupt a superior officer and yet also feeling awkward over whether they should speak, or say something, anything. After another minute had passed and *Oberführer* Richter's stein remained in mid-air like he was going to clink it with another stein and say *"prost"* at any moment, Johannes finally stepped in and said, "Our work here in Poland is of the utmost importance, carrying out the Final Solution to the Jewish Question." He took a slight pause then, as if waiting for *Oberführer* Richter to discipline him for having interrupted a senior officer. But when no rebuke came, he continued. "When you consider the tremendous work we've done here these past two months, dealing with the issue of the Hungarian Jews, I'd say we're all deserved of a much needed break and Solahütte provides just that," Johannes finished, taking a huge swig of beer, to which Georg and Oskar banged their steins down on the table before them with a hearty "here here."

"How far away is it?" Max asked, wanting to be polite by seeming interested, but inwardly not interested in the least. He had spent summer and winter holidays in places like the Black Forest and the Bavarian Alps. He highly doubted some rustic lodge in Poland so near to an extermination camp where the air was always thick with smoke could really be described as charming and idyllic. He was here to do a job and now with the invasion of Europe and the Allies wanting to end the war, Max was of the mindset to carry out the incredible vision of *Reichsführer* Himmler, not idle away precious time hiking and sunbathing. But he was the newest member of the SS officer staff and knew he needed to play along, especially if *Oberführer* Richter was gung-ho on going. He had come to Auschwitz to make a name for himself, one that was obtained on his merits alone, not the "good word" his father, *Herr* von Hofmannsthal, could put in for him with the men at *Prinz-Albrecht-Straße* like he had done so many times before.

"What, 29 or so kilometers?" Johannes asked the other men.

"*Ya*," Oskar said. "I don't know about you," he began, his words sounding slightly slurred, undoubtedly from all the beer he had already consumed, "but-" and before he could utter another word, he slumped forward, his head making a loud thump as it hit the wooden table.

"Well, you've no doubt learned by now that Oskar here," Georg said, poking the passed out man on his shoulder, which elicited no reaction, "can't hold his beer. But I personally am looking forward to this weekend immensely. In just eight weeks we've processed what, some 400,000 of them? The Hungarian Jews I mean. Gassed 80 percent of them upon arrival? It's a shame we don't have more crematoria, it's entirely unproductive having to dig those pits and burn the bodies like that."

Georg was referring to the issue that had plagued camp officials for weeks now, the crematoria not being able to handle the large number of deportees who had been immediately gassed upon arriving at Auschwitz. It had gotten to such dire straits that even the Commandment, Höss, had traveled to Budapest to reorganize the transports.

Shortly after coming to Auschwitz Max had been present for one of the Hungarian transports arriving at night. Never before in his life had he witnessed such pitiful displays of humanity. Even during his time in the Soviet Union, the Jews who had met their end exhibited more dignity than these Hungarian Jews, remembering how it wasn't just women and children sobbing, flailing their arms about, but grown men too, as they were separated and carted away to their respective areas. He had been thoroughly disgusted by this scene and was thankful he held a high enough rank that he didn't have to be present for the arrival of transports into the camp unless he wanted to.

By this time, *Oberführer* Richter had gotten up and stumbled to a nearby table, one with even higher-ranking officers than him. Looking cautiously around then, Johannes whispered the one thing they had all been thinking for weeks now, ever since news had reached them about the Normandy invasion. The one thing they were loath to even contemplate, although each of their futures was inextricably tied to it, not to mention it was considered treasonous if one were caught saying the unimaginable-

"What if Germany loses the war?"

❧ CHAPTER 31 ❧

Auschwitz Camp
Oświęcim, Poland
December 1944

He hadn't dared breathe a word of it to any of his fellow officers, not even Georg and Oskar, both of whom he had become incredibly close with, but Max was already planning for his future. One in which if Germany lost the war (which was highly likely from everything he had been reading about the Allies' victories throughout Western Europe, storming through their way through France and Italy, liberating towns and villages as they went, their ultimate goal, of course, to reach Germany), Max was not going to pay the price for having been a soldier, for simply following orders. But he knew the Americans wouldn't see it that way, not with all the Jews that ran their country, who whispered into Roosevelt's ear. And he sure as hell was not going to be taken prisoner by the Red Army and sent to some godforsaken *gulag* in the Soviet Union. He'd rather personally see to Germany's defeat than suffer that fate.

But military intelligence reports said that the Red Army was close to Auschwitz, that it was perhaps a month, maybe more, maybe less, until they reached it. Tentative plans had been discussed to take most of the prisoners and transport them to other camps in Germany, far enough away from the advancing Soviets. It was not officially said but all the officers at the camp, (well, the intelligent ones that is, not the ones who vehemently denied the downfall and any possible capitulation of *der Führer* himself and would challenge you to a duel to defend the Fatherland's honor were it 1744 and not 1944), all knew Germany's military was on the brink of collapse. And so the rationale was that they'd take the prisoners from the camp that was much too close to the front now, and move them to camps inside Germany, using them as forced laborers and thus keeping Germany and its military alive in the fight.

When these plans had initially been presented, Max had, of course, nodded along with his approval and helped to finesse them as the news became grimmer and more serious with reports from the Eastern Front and the continual successes of the bulldozing Soviet army. But secretly he had been hatching his own plan of escape. And he had his old friend Sam Weiss to thank for it.

"Did you always work in the Kanada?" Max asked Sam one night as the latter was clearing the coffee service away from Max's desk.

Head bowed, not in deference to him, Max knew, but more so that Sam didn't have to look at him, he replied, "No, not originally."

"Then where?" Max asked, irritated that Sam insisted on his usual games.

"For a few days, I assisted the tattooist. But the *Oberscharführer* who oversaw the work of the tattooist, he didn't like the look of me, he said I reminded him of some dirty Jew back home in Munich he had dirtied his boots on one day when he had been insolent, so I was removed. Luckily enough I was reassigned to the Kanada and not some outside detail."

"Wait," Max said, his mind trying to process what Sam had just told him. "You tattooed numbers on the prisoners?"

"I mostly assisted, but when large numbers of transports came in and the tattooist was falling behind, yes, I did do a number of the prisoner tattoos," Sam said quietly, almost sounding ashamed for having been the person to have branded the prisoners with their identity numbers. And then in almost a whisper, afraid that he might get hit for what he was about to say, added, "I was glad to have been transferred. I didn't feel right being the one doing that." As if applying a tattoo to an arm was such a heinous action, Max sneered to himself.

"That will be all prisoner 126296," calling Sam by his number, not even in private calling him by the name he had called him his entire life. And just like that, Sam was dismissed as Max started to calculate his escape.

Auschwitz Camp
Oświęcim, Poland
Mid-January 1945

Max rubbed the underside of his left arm, shocked that even days after having dabbed it with a hydrogen tablet, it still felt on fire, his skin still displaying an angry looking shade of red. But it had been worth it, he told himself, his blood type tattoo, what all SS men were required to have marked on them in order to identify their blood type if a transfusion was ever needed while they were unconscious or their dog tag or pay book was missing. It was also a way that Allied soldiers would be able to immediately identify SS men, Johannes had said one night in the officers' dining hall, to mark them apart from the rest, to deal with them the harshest. Georg and Oskar had scoffed at this, saying that Johannes was being ridiculous, that to the Allies, all Germans were Nazis. But later on that night, apart from the rest, Max had asked Johannes if there was anything he could do to get rid of his tattoo. And that's when Johannes told him a suggestion his doctor friend had given-hydrogen tablets. The pain persisted for weeks but within three days, his tattoo had been erased. And were he ever to fall into Allied hands, obviously the irritation on his arm would be long cleared up by then.

"I'm kinda going to miss this place, "said a voice from behind, as Max whirled around to see Oskar standing there, looking off in the distance to where smoke billowed from the crematoria chimneys. "I mean, it's been home to me since what, 1941?" he asked rhetorically since Max had no idea how long the other man had been working here.

"Don't you want to go back to your life? I mean the life you had before the war?" Max asked, tired of hearing Oskar wax lyrically about the wondrous bucolic life that was Auschwitz.

"Are you kidding?" Oskar scoffed in disbelief. "Not at all. As a *Hauptscharführer* I've risen to a rank I can be proud of, one where my poverty on the streets of Hamburg no longer matters. Here I've become somebody, Max."

He stopped talking then but Max knew the rest. That in a world without a place like Auschwitz and the Nazis and the SS and Hitler, he was a nobody without any sort of a future, professionally or financially. So of course he didn't want "this" world to end. To Max, there were too many Oskars already. And he wasn't going to be dragged down by any of them. Let them live in their fantasy world of denial, that the Third Reich would last forever. He knew differently now in these waning days of war.

"There you are," Georg called out as he walked towards both men. "I've just received word that we leave five days from now. But we must get rid of many of the prisoners in the next few days; no sense in taking anybody with us who will just slow us down or cause us to use unnecessary bullets on them," he said laughingly. "We're taking around 60,000 with us. We'll march them towards Wodzisław and from there they'll board freight trains to go to Germany," he said with an air of neat precision, as if they were planning a picnic, and not about to take tens of thousands of sick and starving prisoners on a march in the dead of a Polish winter. What could possibly go wrong, Max thought dryly.

"And even in the face of trial and adversity, we'll continue serving the *führer* with the work that we'll do, bringing the prisoners to Germany to help our military," Oskar said, sounding as if he were one of Jesus' disciples trying to convert the unsuspecting.

And he'll be the first to get captured, tried, and executed, Max thought before excusing himself from his friends and walking away, calculating how he was going to tell Sam about his new job.

"You're going to tattoo me with your camp number."

Sam looked at Max, not comprehending what his former friend had just said.

"I don't understand," Sam said in a wobbly tone.

"You know how to apply the tattoos, you're going to tattoo your number, 126296, on me," Max said evenly.

"But why?" Sam replied, still not getting it.

"It's not your business to ask why. You will do as you're told or I'll shoot you myself," Max said in a cold tone. Months ago that threat wouldn't have worked on his old friend, but now that gossip was rife with talk of the approaching Red Army set to liberate the camp any day, Max knew that threat now did indeed carry some weight. That if he had survived years of the hell that was called

Auschwitz, when so many had been outright killed or died as a result of starvation and disease and cruelty from sadistic guards, he wasn't about to die now so close to freedom.

And so later that night, Sam tattooed the numbers 126296 in blue ink with painstaking precision with a single needle on Max's left forearm. Max had surreptitiously procured the necessary materials earlier that day. The number that had been Sam's identity for more than a year now was a number that the former best friends now shared, uniting them in a most bizarre and unusual manner. If Sam understood Max's ultimate plan, he didn't let on.

Just as Max had feared, the days leading up to the evacuation from the camp, the subsequent disposal of thousands of too weak and infirm prisoners before they left, marching the prisoners they took with them to Wodzisław, had been an absolute nightmare. So many had fallen, which then caused others to stop to help them, which then required bullets to be used when one or both failed to get up and keep moving. An absolute waste of resources, Max had thought with disgust at the time. And then there was the matter of loading the prisoners onto the freight trains, many of the camp guards grumbling about having to help the Jews climb up onto them for they had no strength to do it themselves. But the chaos that ensued, the absolute departure from the tidy order that was German culture, naturally would work to Max's advantage.

He had been assigned to the train that was going to Dachau in southern Germany and made sure that Sam was on that particular transport list. If his plan was to work, he couldn't go anywhere that someone would remotely be able to recognize him, so that immediately ruled out camps like Sachsenhausen and Buchenwald, places near enough to the capital.

Not that Max was going to go all the way to Dachau. No, he would be heading off on his own long before the train reached the camp, along with Sam of course.

Auschwitz Camp
Oświęcim, Poland
Mid-January 1945
(a few nights before the evacuation)

"When the right moment presents itself, you and I are going to go off, separate from the others."

Sam looked at him then with confusion, clearly not comprehending what Max had just told him.

"Go where?" Sam asked, almost sounding like a half-wit, something ten years ago Max would have never thought possible.

"The war will be over soon. It's only a matter of time before Germany falls for good," he told Sam. "The Soviets are pushing rapidly from the east, the Allies from the west, pretty soon they'll meet. They all want to be the ones to capture Berlin, to say they were the triumphant victors who personally ended Hitler's reign of terror, to be written about in history books fondly remembered for all time."

Sam remained quiet still but then asked in a steady voice, "Why take me? If the impending downfall of the Third Reich is as near as you say, then why trouble yourself at all with me when I'm nothing more than a dirty Jew?"

The last word came out as a sneer. Perhaps Sam was even mimicking the numerous times Max had called him that before he had gone to the front. Trying his best to remain nonplussed and not simply blurt out "for leverage, you idiot!" and ruin his place, he said instead, "Because we've been friends since we were babies. Because our mothers were friends, because I was always a part of your family as you were mine."

Looking at him with cold and hardened eyes, Sam said, "We stopped being friends the night you stood by and did nothing as my father was arrested and deported to his death."

And with that, he left Sam's office, not having been dismissed yet by Max and never once looking back at him, as if by doing so he was saying to Max, "go ahead and shoot me."

Would Sam really fight him when the time came for them to run, Max wondered later that evening as he lay in his bed in his quarters, staring up at the ceiling.

For days he had debated whether he should tell Sam his escape plans for the two of them. He wasn't necessarily worried that Sam would tell one of the other prisoners. He'd had *Schüze* Kohler speak to Sam's *Blockälteste*, the barracks leader where Sam slept, and the private had reported that Sam kept to himself, that he didn't really talk or fraternize with any of the other prisoners. This had surprised Max, of course. Sam had always been the more social, more popular of them but then he supposed Auschwitz could change people. He obviously was heartened by this bit of news. It made him feel he had nothing to fear by telling Sam about the plans.

The bigger problem now, he thought, was if Sam would make a scene during the journey, scream out to his fellow officers that Max was deserting, that Max believed it was only a matter of time before the Third Reich would fall for good.

Now what to do about that he wondered, as he drummed his fingers on the wooden edge of his bed over and over-

Ba-da-ba

Ba-da-ba

Ba-da-ba

❧

That right moment for slipping away happened to come sooner than Max had planned, but it was far too perfect an opportunity to let it pass by. When the freight train broke down shortly after crossing over the border into Czechoslovakia, he took it as a sign, that now was his chance to get away unnoticed.

The one and only time he had been present on the tracks to witness the selection of new arrivals, he had watched with amazement at how the people couldn't wait to disembark from the train cars, clawing at others like ravaged animals. (Of course, those who were still alive; he had seen many a bloated corpse being removed too.) But now in January, the people didn't want to leave the relative warmth (he surmised from body heat?) of the cars as opposed to standing out in the cold against the blowing winds and frigid temperatures. Luckily for him, Sam had disembarked and was standing slightly away from the others.

"Will we be here long?" Sam asked Max, his teeth chattering as he spoke.

From within the warmth of his thick and luxuriously lined black, wool greatcoat, Max replied, "They will. They're supposedly trying to call for another train to come. If it doesn't within the next five hours, they'll be going on foot to Dachau."

"But-" Sam started to stammer, "We're nowhere near Germany, it's still hundreds of miles to the German border!" he said angrily. "Our clothes are in tatters, many don't have shoes, many more are sick, and we're all starving and you want us to march to Germany? From where, Czechoslovakia?? If that's even where we actually are?? Was that always your plan? Just kill us on some death march since the gas chambers couldn't do it?"

Gingerly smiling at the other man, Max said, "Sam, did you not hear me the first time? I said 'they.' **They** will be here at the Czech border for however long it takes, **they** will be marching to Dachau if no train can be procured. You and I will be long gone by then," displaying as wide and mischievous a smile as the Cheshire Cat.

And then he added, "By all means, if you really want to stay here and embark on some 'death march' as you called it, die along the side of a rural road in Czechoslovakia, buried in some pit where no one will ever know what happened to you, then by all means, remain here. Please," Max added with an extra dose of sinister sweetness to his voice. "But if you wish to live, to start a new life, in America perhaps, then you'll want to come with me."

Max let his words sink in; he could see Sam's thoughts running through his head deciphering what Max had just uttered. His words were of course baseless. He needed Sam. His plan would not work without the other man, the Jew prisoner from one of the death camps, as the Allied media were calling them, being with him. Until Sam was no longer needed. For the simple truth of the matter, all Jews served some purpose but all Jews were also expendable.

"I'll go."

Of course you will thought Max, relishing the sound of those two little words.

❧ CHAPTER 32 ❧

German countryside
February 1945

"Here," Max, said throwing a tiny notebook into Sam's lap. "Start writing down everything about your family-when your parents were born, the names of your grandparents, years they were born, years they married, where they married, where they lived, how many children they had, what they did for work, that kind of stuff."

"Are you joking?" Sam said, not bothering to look up, but rather looking down at his hands which like the rest of him, were sallow in color. They were the same age, both 24, and yet Sam easily looked as if he were 10, maybe 15 years older than Max.

"Do I look like I'm joking?" Max screamed at Sam, not caring in the least if their hosts for the night heard him.

For weeks now, they had been traveling west, going in the direction of Germany. Before they had left Auschwitz, Max had stolen a uniform of a camp guard, the *SS-Totenkopfverbände* which he'd had Sam change into once they had fled. When the other man had wanted to bury his camp rags, Max had stopped him from doing so, saying he'd hold onto them, that they might come in handy along their journey. Since members of the *SS-Totenkopfverbände* were also considered full members of the Waffen-SS, he thought the uniform was plausible enough to not arouse any suspicion. The Death's Head collar patch usually could be relied on to induce fear in people. And what's more, many would not even know the difference.

The story Max had concocted if they were stopped was that they had gotten separated from the regiment on the Eastern Front and were fleeing west to escape the advancing Red Army, lest they be taken as prisoners of war and sent to some Soviet *gulag*.

Finding a place to sleep each night had become infinitely easier since reaching Germany. Czechoslovakia had at times been trying until Sam had opened his mouth one night to a farmer there and starting conversing to him in Czech! Max had been shocked that his friend was speaking a Slavic language. He knew Sam spoke some French and English (better than he did), but Czech? When Max asked how he had come to speak it, he had just said, "one of the other prisoners" and then rolled over and fell fast asleep. Max was silently enraged at Sam's insolence but mentally chided himself to bide his time, that soon enough he'd be rid of the Jew.

There had been a few nights, even since arriving in Germany, where people had looked at them with suspicion. They didn't for a moment believe that Sam, with his shaved head whose hair was growing in patches erratically now and his sallow looking skin, had been in the SS. Not when you compared him to how relatively healthy and robust Max looked. To shut them up, Max just said, "lice," and that had them scurrying away, never once bothering them after leaving a chunk of bread and cheese and some salt pork if they miraculously had any (which typically they did not).

"I just don't know if I can remember all of my family," Sam said quietly, any levity his tone had conveyed just a moment earlier vanishing.

"Do your best," Max said icily and walked away.

German countryside
Wednesday, March 28 1945

"Sunday is Easter," the old lady said to him, smiling, showing her two missing front teeth as if she were a schoolgirl of eight and not 80. Max painfully smiled back. The old woman and her husband were dressed in the traditional attire of Bavaria, he in *lederhosen*, she in *dirndl* as if they were about to perform some folkloric dance for a captive audience. But their audience comprised only Max and Sam, neither of whom were particularly desirous of a musical revue, let alone non-stop chitchat.

But Max couldn't overly complain, for this couple was the kindest and most gracious they had encountered since they had begun their journey in the desolation of Czechoslovakia. In fact, when Max had said they were utterly exhausted, the old man had implored them to stay a few days at their decrepit mountain hamlet, the old woman bobbing her head in acquiescence, the snow-white braids that rested on top of her head moving as she did.

"This Sunday you say?" Max asked, the wheels in his head starting to move.

"*Ya*," the woman replied, her braids bobbing enthusiastically once more.

Sam stared at Max uncomprehendingly, clearly confused as to Max's sudden interest in the Easter holiday, for just as Sam's family hadn't been overly religious Jews, Max's parents hadn't been overly religious Christians.

German countryside
Thursday, March 29 1945

Just as the train breaking down at the Czechoslovakian border had provided Max with the sign he needed on when to desert, finding out it was Holy Week was the newest sign from Providence.

Tomorrow is the day, Max thought to himself, watching Sam fitfully sleep on the cot next to him.

German countryside
Friday, March 30 1945
Good Friday

"Come on," Max whispered to Sam's sleeping form, roughly shaking him awake.

"What?" Sam asked groggily, looking around in confusion.

"We're leaving now, gather your things," he ordered.

"But why?" Sam asked, his voice still thick with sleep. "I thought we were going to stay and rest a few more days."

"Because I said so," Max hissed at him.

Knowing not to argue any further, Sam did as he was told and within five minutes they were out the door of the tiny wooden cabin, the old couple clearly oblivious to their departure. Max swiped a couple of apples and some stale dark bread from their larder.

They had been walking for a couple of hours when Max purposely fell behind. He slowly removed his Luger from his front pants pocket, careful to not make a sound so as to alert Sam.

It was only when he cocked the pistol, the unmistakable sound of the hammer being pulled back, the round being loaded into the chamber, that Sam realized what was happening, stopped, and slowly turned around.

Sam's face was expressionless. No trace of anger, or shock, or sadness, devoid of any emotion except a knowing understanding of what was about to come.

"Jesus was crucified today. So I thought it's only fitting that today's the day you die too, one more Jew to join Jesus wherever that may be. "And with that, Max fired his pistol, aiming it directly at Sam's heart.

CHAPTER 33

Pittsburgh, Pennsylvania
2006

"It was only years later I learned that in 1945, Passover fell over Easter. So I gave the Jew a most fitting and appropriate end," Becky's father said.

"The Jew." She heard the words echoing back in her head. Becky stared at him with open revulsion and horror, her mind unable to process the multitude of unimaginable tragedies and horrors she had just listened to for the past three hours.

But she needed to hear, to know the rest of the sordid story that he built lie after lie.

"What happened next?" she asked.

"What, you mean after I killed him?"

"Yes."

"I continued to move, continued to make use of the power and freedom my SS uniform brought me. By that point, few people, few Germans that is, were overly concerned about a potential deserter. Most knew the Reich was over, done with, and simply wanted to return to a life where there were no more shortages and privations. But when there was talk that the Americans were close to Dachau, in southern Germany, close to liberating it, I knew my time had come to enact my plan."

"Your plan?"

"My plan to become Samuel Weiss, former prisoner of Auschwitz who escaped his captors during the death march. I ate next to nothing, I crudely shaved my hair, and of course, I already had my camp number," her father said, holding up his left arm as if to proudly display it. "By the time I made it to Dachau at the end of April, I looked the part of an escaped prisoner who had been hiding out in the wilderness for months."

"You weren't worried that someone would recognize you?"

"There wasn't a soul who would have been able to definitively say, yes, that's Maximilian von Hofmannsthal, by just looking at me. And the camp number? Absolutely not. And besides, by that time, any of the high-ranking SS officers would have long since fled the camps, even though most got picked up shortly after by the Americans. Their SS blood type tattoo always gave them away. You see, the American doctors, well I suppose the British and Soviet doctors too, were trained to look for those."

"Were you ever in a displaced persons camp? Or was that just another one of your lies?"

"Of course I was!" he said angrily, clearly offended she would think such a thing. "I spent four and a half years living in Föhrenwald, a total shithole that the Americans ran. Utterly horrific conditions, not enough food, armed guards everywhere you turned, a total nightmare."

Was she dreaming this or was her father really saying these things? An SS officer complaining about the conditions in a displaced persons camp and yet there weren't senseless killings or people being gassed at those.

"Where was this Föhrenwald," she asked him, not familiar with the name.

"Wolfratshausen. In Bavaria, in southern Germany."

"How could you pass off being Jewish? You didn't know any Hebrew. Did you even know any of the customs or what any of the high holy days meant?"

"Why do you think I had Sam with me for as long as I did? I didn't just have him write down all those names of people and dates. I had him teach me about your Rosh Hashanah and Hanukkah and seders. Not that he was any great Judaic scholar," he said snidely. "So it was easy enough to feign the part of the rich, unobservant Berlin Jew. But as I said already, Samuel Weiss was my ticket to **my** becoming Samuel Weiss."

Becky stopped short at the mention of 'your.' As if the past 61 years no longer mattered, as if he were the cruel and sadistic 24 year old SS officer once more standing here in the house of her mother.

Her mother. "Mom suspected, didn't she?" Becky asked, already knowing the answer.

"She never outright confronted me about it, but yes, she suspected something, that I wasn't truly who I said I was. Do I think she thought I was an SS officer who oversaw the operations of a Polish death camp? I doubt it. Your mother was too naïve and stupid a soul to be so methodical in her thinking.

"So my dear, my very own *mischling*, what do you intend to do with this bit of news? Turn me in? Your very own *vater*? The headlines that would make," he chuckled as he slowly sat back down. "Not to mention, I doubt your mother's side of the family would want anything to do with you once they heard you were half-Nazi, so you'd indeed be all alone in this world."

What should she do. The question had plagued her for months now, a mental torment that had started thousands of miles across a wide ocean in a land whose history and culture ran through her blood. She had come up with a couple of different scenarios, one of them being she simply walked away from him, removed him entirely from her life. But she knew that wouldn't really work, that for the rest of her life, for as long as he lived, she would harbor the guilt knowing that she had done nothing. And even once he was dead, the memory of him and his evil past would still haunt her, that he had gotten to live life as an old man while millions had not. And then there was the scenario of anonymously contacting the authorities and turning him in. But on reflection that seemed too easy and too clean a break with him, like she was letting others handle her mess. So she thought of the only thing that truly made logical sense to her.

"You have one week to go to the authorities, to go on your own volition, to go with some semblance of dignity and respect towards your victims. That even though you have lived 'free' for over 60 years, at this stage of your life, you are finally doing the right thing, to pay a very small price for the millions of lives you took, for causing everlasting pain for the millions of people who survived whose lives would never be the same."

"And if I don't?" her father challenged her.

"Then I will go to the authorities myself and turn you in. But I am giving you the opportunity to do the right thing when so many of your kind did not, to pay for your sins."

And with that she left, walking out into the cold night air, her heart and head feeling infinitely clearer.

Five days later when Becky went to his house after being unable to reach him by phone for the past two days, she found him dead, his lifeless body slumped over in his desk chair, the German Luger still in his left hand, his camp tattoo number on display.

Even in death he had challenged her and won this round. He had left a suicide note, claiming that he was forgetting more and more things and did not want to be a "burden" on his daughter when his condition became more severe, that he had led a long and fruitful life but now wanted to be reunited with his wife and parents and sister. There, of course, was no official diagnosis of anything having to do with Alzheimer's or even general dementia. But he knew his daughter. He knew Becky would not request any official autopsy with his advanced age. So his sudden death would be plausible and believed by all.

But Becky won in finality. He had left no burial instructions in his will. And so she had his body cremated, adamant that Maximilian von Hofmannsthal would not desecrate the Jewish cemetery where her mother was buried by having him interred alongside her. When people asked, she had lied and said it's what he'd wanted, that he didn't want any sort of burial or final resting place. Because that's what he truly deserved.

 EPILOGUE

Berlin, Germany
October 2009

"Babe? You ready?"

"I'll just be a minute," Becky called back to Adam through the closed door of their hotel room's bathroom.

Adam had surprised Becky with a trip to Germany, Berlin to be exact. He knew how much she had wanted to return, both to pay respect to the real Sam and his family, but also for closure for herself, to finally come to terms with the tainted and evil blood she carried through her veins. It had meant so much to Becky that Adam wanted to accompany her on this emotional journey, to help in finally closing this painful chapter of her life.

For the last few years, Becky had spent hours researching the Weiss family tree, examining everything from the *das Jüdische Adressbuch von 1931* (the Jewish Directory of 1931) to the *Gedenkbuch. Opfer der Verfolgung der Juden unter der nationalsozialistischen Gewaltherrschaft in Deutschland 1933-1945* (a memorial book listing the victims of the persecution of the Jews in Germany under the Nazis) to even having many cyber exchanges back and forth with a kind archivist at the Centrum Judaicum at the Neue Synagogue. It was through these endeavors that she was ultimately put in touch with a Uri Bitton of Israel, son of Rebekah Bitton, nee Weiss, who had immigrated to what was then British Palestine in 1928. The same person who Becky and Adam were going to meet today outside of the long since rebuilt building on *Kroenstraße,* the same place where Becky's father had grown up and where Uri's cousins and aunt and uncle had once lived.

Becky had debated how much she should tell Uri. As Adam and Minah always reminded her, she was not to pay or should have to atone for the sins of her father. And yet she had wanted to meet this Uri, to meet the only remaining physical tie to Samuel Weiss. So she had decided to tell him some of the truth, that her grandmother, Hildegard von Hofmannsthal, had risked her life during the war to help save those of his cousins, regardless of the dangers posed to her. How she would die all alone during the Battle of Berlin, her body never recovered, presumably buried in some unmarked mass grave along with the thousands of other civilians who perished in one of the last major offensives of the European Theater during the war. She would not tell him how her grandfather, a high-ranking official at the *Deutsche Reichsbahn,* Germany's national railway company, which conveyed three million Jews to their ultimate deaths at the six extermination camps during the war, was never held to account for the deportations. One of so many German collaborators and Nazi criminals who never paid for the crimes they sowed against the Jews all those years. Becky had no idea if he had led a happy life after the war, but he had led a long one, not passing away until 1984 according to the obituary she had found online.

No, Becky spoke fondly of her grandmother, because it was her blood that ran through her, the one von Hofmannsthal she could truly be proud of. Becky only wished she could have met her, or at least seen a picture of what she looked like.

Opening the door, Becky saw Adam standing there, waiting for her. She had never loved him more than at that very moment. The one man who truly believed in her, every last bit.

"Ready," she said, smiling broadly at him.

As they approached the corner of *Kroenstraße* and *Charlottenstraße*, Becky could see an elderly man standing there, his arm laced through that of a younger woman's, presumably his daughter. What was her name Becky thought, trying to remember the very exotic name Uri had mentioned a couple of times in his emails, the child who would be accompanying him on the trip. Alona? Adama?

"Rebekah?" the man asked in flawless English as they stopped to stand in front of him.

She had a flashback of her father then and his insistence her entire life of calling her Rebekah and not Becky as she insisted he do, the many stupid fights that had ensued as a result of both their determined persistence and outright stubbornness. She was about to say "please call me Becky," but thought better of it, knowing how much the name Rebekah must mean to him.

"Yes, it's so nice to finally meet you face to face after all this time, Mr. Bitton," Becky said. "And this is my boyfriend, Adam Lefkovitz."

Becky could have sworn that Uri's eyes lit up at the mention of Adam's very clearly Jewish last name.

"And this," Uri began turning towards the younger woman at his side, "is my daughter Alya," he said.

Alya. I knew it started with an 'a' Becky half smiled, to which Adam gave her a look that read "What's so funny?" She mouthed back the word "later" to him.

"She wouldn't hear of me traveling to Germany all by myself," Uri stated half in jest, half in earnest, Becky thought. "I mean, she won't even let me go to the beach by myself and I live right across the street!" he exclaimed in mock horror, his bushy white eyebrows rising comically as he said this.

"My dear papa," Alya said, looking at him with warm, loving eyes, "likes to think he's still a young 20 year old in the Israeli Army and not the 79 year old grandfather he actually is," to which all four of them laughed. "Besides, it is the job of daughters to worry about their papas," she added, to which he responded by kissing her lightly on the cheek.

"And the job of papas to be forever grateful that they were blessed with a daughter such as you."

So this is what it must be like to be loved by one's father Becky thought as she watched the father and daughter before her. Sensing her discomfort Adam cut in and asked, "So, when were the *stolpersteine* installed?" bringing the conversation back to why they were there in the first place.

"In 2001," Uri said quietly. "What would have been my Uncle Sam's 80th birthday had he lived. I only wish my mother could have been there for it. She never got over losing her entire family, never forgave herself for not doing more to try to save them."

They paused then, Becky looking down at Sam's stumbling block, remembering the man who had brought these complete strangers from opposite sides of the world together here in Berlin, where a long time ago in another world, another life that was long since forgotten, each of their families had once happily lived.

"What are the flowers you have there?" Alya asked, pointing to the bouquet of flowers that Becky held in her right hand.

"Cornflowers," Becky answered. "They were my mother's favorite," her voice slightly catching. She had wanted to lay flowers of some kind at the *Kroenstraße* address, adjacent to the four *stolpersteine* for the Weiss family. Becky had no idea what her grandmother's favorite flower had been but she liked to imagine that she would have liked the beautiful cornflower as much as her own mother had, and that had they known each other, perhaps they would have even been good friends, Judy being as dear to Hildegard as Samuel's sister Marta had once been. She laid the bouquet on the pavement then, closing her eyes for a moment to remember her brave and righteous grandmother and then lightly ran her fingers over each of the four *stolpersteine*.

"They're absolutely lovely," Alya said, smiling at Becky as she stood back up.

Her father nodded at her and then Alya removed from her purse a small wrapped parcel which she handed to Becky.

"My mother was not one for fancy clothes or furnishings. I mean she moved to Palestine and lived on a *kibbutz* for 15 years," to which father and daughter quietly laughed while Becky and Adam just smiled at each other. "She took some books with her, well, it was her brother Benjamin who was more the scholar she'd always say, but what she did take were droves and droves of photographs, her most precious things in life she'd say. Even during her 'sad spells' as she called them, she was still taking pictures, her Brownie camera always in her hands as if it were attached. Her photographs were the only thing she had left of an entire family that was taken from her."

Becky's heart felt full at the mention of this, remembering the many photographs Uri had sent her in the beginning so she could see what Sam and Marta and even their parents had looked like.

Continuing on he said, "After she passed, I looked through her photographs, I mean there were hundreds upon hundreds of them. Very few were dated but many had names on them, names that meant nothing to me at the time. But once we started talking and I learned more about you, your family, I looked back through them and came across this," he said just as Becky had finished removing the parchment paper to reveal a small box.

Taking off the lid she looked down to see inside a black and white photograph of two beautiful women, sitting on a park bench, outfitted in summer dresses and chic hats.

"Turn it over," he said quietly.

Her hands slightly shaking, she did and saw inscribed in faded but neat script the words-

Giselle und Hildegard
Tiergarten, Juni 1926

Giselle Weiss and Hildegard von Hofmannsthal. Hildegard, her courageous grandmother who had done the right thing at a time so many did not. And it was only then that Becky allowed herself to finally cry.

"I remember you saying you had no idea what your grandmother looked like, that you had never even seen a picture of her," Uri said.

"*Danke*," she told him looking up at him through her tears of happiness. "*Danke schön.*"

Author's Note

I have the infamous and long running 2019-2020 French pension reform strike to thank for why I randomly and unexpectedly ended up in cold and dreary Berlin, Germany one early December. Originally I was supposed to spend 3.5 weeks in the southern French city of Montpellier working on my *passé composé* in between downing copious amounts of *rosé* wine and playing the part of tourist each weekend, jetting off to various corners of the country, all the while documenting it on Instagram. Well, said strike put a major dent in those plans and rather than be incredibly unhappy and depressed over things like train cancellations and nonrefundable hotel reservations, I decided life was too short to be that unhappy and decided to visit Amsterdam and Berlin, two European capitals I had never been to before.

Even though I wasn't adequately dressed (I had brought with me a coat that was perfectly suited for the south of France, not northern Europe) and caught a cold along the frigid and long train journey from Amsterdam to Berlin (European train travel can be grossly overrated), I ended up falling in love with the German capital. It doesn't have the romantic allure of a city like Paris or the timeless invitation of a place like London but it does have history, loads and loads of it. And for this history loving nerd, it was pure bliss.

My inspiration for the story behind *The Dead are Resting* actually came from a visit to the Topography of Terror Museum. Like the character of Becky, I visited on a cold and dark night where there was a light rain falling, and like her, I couldn't help but feeling spooked walking the relatively deserted streets from my hotel on Potsdamer Platz to the museum and imagining the extreme terror people must have felt when they were arrested and taken to the Gestapo Headquarters on what was then *Prinz-Albrecht-Straße*. It was later renamed *Niederkirchnerstraße* by the post-war German government due to the former's connotation with Nazi Germany. (Note: The Topography of Terror's current building didn't open until 2010 even though in the book the character of Becky visits it in 2006 on her trip to Germany. I changed this for the benefit of the storyline.)

There were many haunting photographs that stood out to me on my visit, but the ones that stuck with me and haunted me long after I left were those of the laughing Auschwitz camp officials, frolicking as if they were simply on a summer holiday and not indirectly overseeing the systematic murdering of one million people. I say ones because "the" photo from my novel was from a collection of photographs taken by Karl Höcker, the adjutant to the final camp commandant at Auschwitz, who had taken them to have as "personal keepsakes." Today, Höcker's album, which has been dubbed "Laughing at Auschwitz" (for all the photos in it are of laughing and smiling subjects) is owned by the United States Holocaust Memorial Museum in Washington D.C. It was donated by a retired United States Army intelligence officer who had come across it in Frankfurt, Germany.

The album contains many famous figures and war criminals like Josef Mengele, aka the Angel of Death, and Rudolf Höss, the longest-serving commandant of the Auschwitz camp. The discovery and subsequent publication of the album was huge because it was the first time Nazis at leisure at Auschwitz was shown. In addition, the album contained eight photographs of Mengele, some of the few in existence of the camp's infamous doctor during the time he spent at the most horrific extermination camp. But most of the people in the album's photographs are unknown, nameless, never to be identified, for who would ever reveal that they or their fathers or mothers or grandparents were one of those people in the photos? One of those people directly or indirectly responsible for the deaths of more than a million people? Who were having daily sing-alongs and laughing gaily while less than 20 miles away people were being gassed to death and dying from starvation and disease.

And if you're curious as to why I use the word "indirectly" above, the 2011 conviction of John Demjanjuk by German courts as an accessory to 28,000 murders at Sobibor extermination camp in Poland while he served as a Nazi guard there during World War II set a completely new legal precedent in Germany. Prior to the trial of Demjanjuk, it was extremely difficult for German prosecutors to convict former Nazi camp guards, as they were required to find a specific act of murder to charge them with. They needed specifics like the date and time of a particular crime and naturally such evidence against individual camp guards was difficult to produce. As such, there was a very low conviction rate for death camp guards. However, once Demjanjuk was convicted, Germany actively began going after and prosecuting former death camp guards since the court ruling had proved that simply from having "been" at a camp, you were complicit in the murder of six million people. And then in 2019, German prosecutors began charging guards who had "worked" at concentration camps (as opposed to death camps) since even if the outright extermination of the Jews at concentration camps wasn't the intended purpose, thousands still died as a result of starvation, sickness and disease, and acts of cruelty from camp guards. A line from a *New York Times* article by Rick Rojas and Richard Fausset from March 7, 2020 on Nazi hunters perfectly sums up the importance of the Demjanjuk precedent-

> *"They were part of the SS machinery of oppression that kept concentration camp prisoners in atrocious conditions of confinement."*

Most camp guards would not go on to become notorious on a global level and have a world renowned actor like Gregory Peck portray one of them as he did of Josef Mengele in *The Boys from Brazil*. Yet the camp guards, the "average" individuals, were the cogs to the operation. So the idea came to me that I could write a story around one of the photographs from this infamous album, that I could bring to life a story centered around one of these nameless real-life monsters.

The Dead are Resting is first and foremost a work of fiction but some of the people and events mentioned in it are real. There really were Otto Fassbenders, Jews who worked with the Gestapo during World War II by exposing and denouncing fellow Jews who were living underground with false identities. Jews usually became "catchers" after being arrested themselves and then avoided deportation to a concentration camp by agreeing to hunt down Jews who were posing as non-Jews. Catchers typically received a fixed amount for each Jew they betrayed and brought to the Nazis. The most famous of the Jew catchers was Stella Kübler, who used her blond hair and blue eyes to her advantage in turning in between 600 and 3,000 fellow Jews in Berlin. After being arrested and agreeing to work as a catcher, Kübler had been promised by the Nazis that her parents wouldn't be deported, only for both them and her first husband to be deported to camps and killed. She must not have cared for him too much as her second husband was not only a Jew but also a fellow catcher.

SS officials really did play football with the skulls from graves at the oldest Jewish cemetery in Berlin they had desecrated as Becky learned from Ursula, the kind, elderly German Jewish woman who befriended her over a shared plate of *apfelstrudel* and *zwetschgenknoedel*. And Jewish people who had been arrested and were awaiting deportation really did witness this horrific spectacle from inside the detention center.

The character of Yva, Sam's mother's friend, really did exist and was one of the most famous photographers in Germany during the 1920s and 30s, no small feat considering that photography had historically always been a man's field. She tragically was deported east by the Nazis along with her husband in 1942 and is believed to have been killed upon arrival at the Majdanek death camp in Poland, although there never was an official record of her death. *Stolpersteine* for both Yva and her husband can be found at *Schlüterstraße 45* in the German capital.

And more than a year after the war in Europe had officially ended with Germany surrendering to the Allies, there really was a pogrom in the Polish city of Kielce on July 4, 1946 just like the character of Minah had survived. In a country where the Holocaust claimed the lives of three million Jews (half of ALL Jews killed during the Holocaust), 42 more were killed during this pogrom and more than 40 were wounded in an outbreak of violence carried out by Polish soldiers, police, and civilians against the Jewish community center's gathering of Jewish refugees. This horrific wave of violence against the survivors all started from unfounded rumors of a Christian boy's kidnapping by Jews. It was this pogrom that caused most of the small number of remaining Polish Jews who had survived the Holocaust to flee the country for good.

As for Solahütte, this recreation resort a mere 20 miles from the gas chambers of Auschwitz, really did exist. It was built by prisoners at Auschwitz (some survivors said its construction was just as tough as life in the notorious death camp) so the Nazis had somewhere to go and relax on the weekends since travel home was too far. Also, high-ranking officials wanted to limit contact between camp officers and guards and the local Polish population, thus curtailing any possible slip of the tongue to curious locals about what was really taking place within the confines of Auschwitz. Activities there for SS men and *Helferinnen* (female volunteer typists and clerks of the extermination camp) ranged from hunting, hiking, sunbathing, and excursions to the nearby lake and peaks.

The resort operated from 1940 until it was closed down just before the Red Army liberated Auschwitz in January 1945. It enjoyed a most picturesque setting, situated on a hill by the bend of a river, a beacon of relaxing tranquility. The SS men who went there honestly believed they were deserving of a break from the killings they were orchestrating and overseeing. Going to Solahütte, to this resort, the SS men, often along with their wives and children, had a way to enjoy themselves, because in their sick and sadistic mindsets, their work at Auschwitz was justified and as the expression goes, "just another day at the office."

The main lodge building of the resort was demolished in 2011. Today there is a tavern with most everything else being reclaimed by nature.

I wrote this book for a variety of reasons but one of them being my (very) small part in helping to never forget what I consider to be modern history's darkest time. The number of Holocaust survivors continues to dwindle each passing year. The majority of them now are in their 80s and 90s, and there will come a point in the near future when there will be no survivors left to tell their stories firsthand. Holocaust deniers have always existed but a lack of knowledge about this darkest time is equally alarming. A 2020 survey commissioned by the Conference on Jewish Material Claims Against Germany and administered to millenials and Generation Z participants in all 50 of the United States showed that many were unclear about **basic facts** of the Holocaust, including that they did not know that six million Jews were murdered (half of those thought the death toll was fewer than two million) and that half of the respondents couldn't name one single concentration camp or ghetto even though 400,000 had been established. By not knowing the basic facts about this horrific period of modern history, we are forgetting about and erasing the memory of not only those six million who died, but also the survivors.

The Holocaust is never an easy or pleasant topic to read or talk about, but it's imperative all the same that we do so, that we **always remember and never forget.**

The real-life photograph

"Nazi officers and female auxiliaries (Helferinnen) pose on a wooden bridge in Solahütte. The man on the right carries an accordion."

Solahütte, [Upper Silesia; Auschwitz] Poland-July 1944

Photo Credit:

34585A, The Hoecker Album, United States Holocaust Memorial Museum Archives, Washington D.C.
(Used with permission)

Recommended Reading

I first started reading about the Holocaust when I was in elementary school, simply because I wanted to and not because of assigned readings. My interest in this horrific period in modern history only increased as I grew older, especially since it was never a topic taught in any great detail in the American school system.

I know for many people, the idea of reading about concentration camps and the topic of genocide in general is too upsetting. So that's why I encourage you to read a book written by a Holocaust survivor but from their perspective as a child during World War II. The upsetting and unimaginable horrors are still there, but they're written through the eyes of a child who survived the unthinkable, whose childhood innocence was forever taken away due to the "mad man" of Europe. The titles I list below are strong and powerful reads even if they are children's books. But as a librarian, I can tell you that some of my favorite reads as an adult are those intended for a children's audience but read through the eyes and mind of a grown-up (some are works of fiction but based on actual events).

I purposely am not including *The Diary of Anne Frank* on this list because she's typically the best-known writer of the Holocaust and many people seem to forget (or not even realize) that there were countless child survivors, many of whom wrote their own memoirs.

- *Helga's Diary: A Young Girl's Account of Life in a Concentration Camp* by Helga Weiss (I learned about Helga when I visited the Terezin Concentration Camp in the Czech Republic)
- *Touch Wood: A Girlhood in Occupied France* by Renee Roth-Hano
- *Kindertransport* by Olga Levy Drucker
- *I Have Lived a Thousand Years: Growing Up in the Holocaust* by Livia Bitton-Jackson
- *The Devil in Vienna* by Doris Orgel
- *The Devil's Arithmetic* by Jane Yolen
- *Upon the Head of the Goat: A Childhood in Hungary 1939-1944* by Aranka Siegal (the one Holocaust memoir that's always remained with me)
- *Hedy's Journey: The True Story of a Hungarian Girl Fleeing the Holocaust* by Michelle Bisson (this is a picture book, somewhat of a rarity in Holocaust literature)
- *The Search* by Eric Heuvel (this is a graphic novel, another rarity, set in Nazi-occupied Netherlands during the Holocaust)
- *Rose Blanche* by Christophe Gallaz (another picture book)
- *The Cage: a Holocaust Memoir* by Ruth Minsky Sender
- *We Are Witnesses: Five Diaries of Teenagers Who Died in the Holocaust* by Jacob Boas

Although I briefly touch on the Holocaust in the former Soviet Union in *The Dead Are Resting,* it's by and large very much an unknown topic for many, even those with a fair amount of knowledge regarding the genocide of the Jews. But it should be stated that the USSR was second only to Poland as the country with the highest number of Jewish victims. In addition, most of the Soviet victims of the Holocaust did not die in camps but rather were shot and thrown in mass graves known as killing sites, often near to their homes in what's been called "the Holocaust by bullets." Much about the topic of the Holocaust in Nazi-occupied Soviet territories remained unknown for decades because the Soviet government systematically denied that Jews were specific targets of the Nazi horrors. No monuments or memorials were ever erected over mass execution sites during the existence of the Soviet Union. It's only been since the collapse of the Soviet Union that the world has been able to learn more about the Nazi atrocities that were carried out there, even though denial and harsh resistance to these "truth seekers" often makes their work dangerous. If you are interested in learning more about this particular area of the Holocaust, I strongly recommend these two titles-

- *I Want You To Know We're Still Here: A Post-Holocaust Memoir* by Esther Safran Foer (Safran is the daughter of two Ukrainian Jews who survived the Holocaust but had their entire *shtetls* completely erased from history with the loss of nearly the entire Jewish population by the Nazis and local collaborators)
- *The Holocaust by Bullets: A Priest's Journey to Uncover the Truth Behind the Murder of 1.5 Million Jews* by Father Patrick Desbois and Paul A. Shapiro (Father Desbois has made it his life's work to identify and examine all of the sites where Jews were murdered by Nazi death squads in Ukraine before and during World War II).

These were some of the many sources that were invaluable in researching this book:

Aktives Museum. "Final Sale. The End of Jewish Owned Businesses in Nazi Berlin." *Issuu*, 2010, www.issuu.com/vv_www/docs/katalogvv__engl_web_130dpi.

Brostoff, Anita. *Flares of Memory: Stories of Childhood During the Holocaust*. Oxford, Oxford University Press, 2002.

Burstin, Barbara. *Jewish Pittsburgh*. Charleston, Images of America, 2015.

Cole, Diane. "A Final Effort to Find Nazi War Criminals." *National Geographic*, 10 May 2013, www.nationalgeographic.com/news/2013/5/130507-nazi-war-criminal-holocaust-auschwitz-hans-lipschis-simon-wiesenthal-center-demjanjuk/.

Gross, Leonard. *The Last Jews in Berlin*. New York, Basic Books, 1999.

Guttentag, Gedalia. "Last Voices of Kristallnacht." *Mishpacha Magazine*, 31 October 2018, www.mishpacha.com/last-voices-of-kristallnacht/.

Holzel, David. "My Squirrel Hill." *Washington Jewish Week*, 5 December 2018, www.washingtonjewishweek.com/49994/my-squirrel-hill/editorial-opinion/forum/.

Kohl, Paul. *111 Places in Berlin-On the Trail of Nazis*. Cologne, Emons Publishers, 2014.

Kolbert, Elizabeth. "The Last Trial: A great-grandmother, Auschwitz, and the arc of Justice." *The New Yorker*, 9 February 2015, www.newyorker.com/magazine/2015/02/16/last-trial.

Rojas, Rick and Richard Fausset. "The Mission to Hunt Nazis Has Become a Race Against Time." *The New York Times*, 7 March 2020, www.nytimes.com/2020/03/07/us/Friedrich-Karl-Berger-nazi-guard.html.

Rosenkranz, Halina. "Scars of the Past-Group Work with Holocaust Survivors and Descendants." *Kavod*, Issue 5, Spring 2015, 31 March 2015. www.kavod.claimscon.org/2015/03/scars-of-the-past-group-work-with-holocaust-survivors-and-descendants/.

Stern, Barbara Burstin. *After the Holocaust: The Migration of Polish Jews and Christians to Pittsburgh*. Pittsburgh, University of Pittsburgh Press, 1989.

Author Photo by Barbara Stitzer Photography

Julie Tulba is the author of *The Tears of Yesteryear*. When she's not traveling the world, she calls Pittsburgh, Pennsylvania home. For more information, please visit her website, www.julietulba.com.

Made in the USA
Middletown, DE
19 October 2021